ORDERED MURDER

NANA REVAZISHVILI

authorHOUSE®

AuthorHouse™ UK
1663 Liberty Drive
Bloomington, IN 47403 USA
www.authorhouse.co.uk
Phone: UK TFN: 0800 0148641 (Toll Free inside the UK)
UK Local: (02) 0369 56322 (+44 20 3695 6322 from outside the UK)

Published by AuthorHouse 10/19/2021

ISBN: 978-1-6655-9255-0 (sc)
ISBN: 978-1-6655-9256-7 (e)

Illustrator: Zaal Sulakauri
Proofreader: Natalie Davis

Print information available on the last page.

CONTENTS

Mzia Kvirikashvili-Lawrence
Translator

Ronald Lawrence
Editor-consultant

Nana Revazishvili

"If you do not find a documentary style clear detective in my work, it means that I have not been able to avoid life events or personalities who met me on this road. I tried to support the honest and irreproachable people and compare these with people, living in immoral ways and I have named them all with legal terminology. And now, it is your right to evaluate it."

EDITOR-CONSULTANT'S INTRODUCTION, TRANSLATOR'S INTRODUCTION

The main character of the detective is a young investigator, Londa, who lost a precious man, her teacher and best friend, a leader in her professional and private life.

The main theme of the work is the long struggle for justice with the "black world" and the many obstacles to expose the perpetrators in this struggle.

Constant fear and tension. Sleepless nights to achieve the main aim, specially the mother woman's feelings and the complexity of her profession, there are flawless examples of genuine friendship and standing on this path shows characters and principles.

Unexpected scenes, defeats and victories thoughts, plans, bold decisions, fair Principles, analysis and evaluations all these necessary features very nicely concentrated in this excellent work. Londa's personality is an example of what it is like to be a person who serves the most difficult profession of justice.

The work is written in a very light, easy-to-read language for any kind of reader. In my opinion, the presented detective will be very useful for law students and for beginner lawyers. In front of you is a very interesting detective story documentary written by Nino Revazishvili (under the pseudonym Nino Mariamishvili), which can grant you great pleasure.

Ronald Lawrence
Editor-consultant

Mzia Kvirikashvili-Lawrence
Translator

EDITOR-CONSULTANT'S WORD

This detective story of Nana (Nino) Revazishvili describes in great details the harsh and tense events of the nineties in the twentieth century. The most important factor for the work is to unite the practitioner of the Prosecutor's Office with one person, who has been friend with the artistic word for many years. This is the rare case that gives the author a significant advantage and, like oxygen, requires the genre of documentary fiction. Yes, the main character of the detective is the real prototype of the author. Other characters in the work portray real characters too, with only changed surnames.

Thus, Nana Revazishvili's documentary artistic detective is rich in historical and artistic passages, and as such they merge and interchange so naturally, the reader does not feel where the fiction comes from and where the true story ends. We believe that Georgian readers of detective genre (and not only Georgian readers) perceive the events surrounding the fatal murder of the prosecutor to a different degree. The work sharply illustrates the character of the different generations of people involved in the eternal struggle of good and evil, their humanity and patriotism, their wickedness and treachery, their commitment to their professional duty.

So that, in a nutshell, Nana Revazishvili's detective, with the precision of chronicles, embraces a set of facts and artistic generalization of known events.

I wish the author all the best in realizing her plan. Since yet only the first part of her detective work is over. Who knows what her fate and destiny prepares for the investigator Londa? Will she escape alive and will she lead the investigation to the end or she shares fate of her precious former teacher, Mirza Qurdiani.

Only the author can answer these questions! Author, doctor of criminal law, professor, longtime intern at the prosecutor General's Office of Georgia, and a member of the writers' union of Georgia. She has published numerous literary and scientific works. She is a coauthor of prosecution law.

It is also gratifying that Nana Revazishvili's detective work has been translated into English and will soon take its place in the English-speaking world. The translation is made by a UK citizen, a well-known public figure, researcher and translator, Mrs. Mzia Kvirikashvili-Lawrence. We wish further success to the detective's author and its translator too.

Editor-in-chief:
Ioseb Macharashvili

PREFACE

In recent times, unfortunately, detective genre works have rarely been written, and if any, they are mostly made up of random, nonprofessional writers.

Detective "Ordered Murder" is a notable exception in this respect, as the author of the book Nana (Nino) Revazishvili, be sides being a member of the Writers' Union, she is also a Doctor of Law, coauthor of Prosecuting Law and has worked for various positions in the Prosecutor General's Office of Georgia, including state prosecutor. A legally minded detective based on the documentary reality seen through the eyes of a prosecutor, I am sure the reader will receive it with great warmth and interest.

We wish for the detective work and the author the best of luck.

Editor-in-chief:
Temuri Moniava
Doctor of Law, former Deputy Prosecutor General, State Counselor of Justice, Member of the Prosecutor Council.

COMPLETED A LONG SENTENCE

In April, the day of annunciation, the rusty old doors of the prison were opened by the guard, and Jaba was released after fifteen years' imprisonment. He was standing there outside, feeling strange and lonely, thinking what to do, and where to go. He did not even have any chance to visit the city streets. Soon he moved and started walking. But suddenly, he stopped and looked back while thinking. The prison guard, who stood in the doorway, realized that Jaba did not have any money. He caught up to him and gave him five lari to go home. Unfortunately, Jaba did not have either a house or family. Nothing and no one was waiting for him. Suddenly, tears filled his eyes. He tried to use his freedom, it was very difficult though. Everything was so beautiful around him, that he started trembling.

The blue April greeted him with beautiful and refined colours. It was difficult to walk and he had a problem getting his legs to obey him.

He decided to go to the seaside. He could not remember anyone's addresses, nor did he have any relatives. His parents died years ago from grieving about him, and after his parent's death, his only sister changed her identity and emigrated. He did not know about her whereabouts. His only friends are left in prison now. The city was changed so much, he could not believe it, but he knew he was in Batumi. He could not recognize any street there until he arrived at the seaside. He was trying to restore his orientation. Only the sea waves met him like his parents, peacefully and calmly, without storms. The sea reminded him of his childhood. Spent along with his sister and his parents on the beach. He remembered how they used to collect various patterned pebbles, putting them in their t-shirts and carrying happily home.

A woman was on the seashore, looked like his mother. The last time he saw his mother was ten years ago. She was a blue-eyed, pleasant woman, constantly engaged in knitting different patterned socks.

Suddenly, he took out from his heart pocket the only thing that's left from his mother. It was the sock knitted by his mother for him. He kept it all those 15 years, and he just now realized that his mother had not died a decade ago, but now this moment has passed away.

Jaba was forty-seven years old himself now. From the age of thirty-two he was adopted by the walls of prison, and it swallowed his youth. During this time, he even forgot about what he was in prison for.

But was there created a new Jaba, new person? – this was the question.

Was he the person whom the public needed? Or he was the man who was unable to do anything. Despaired, homeless, and monotonous. He left on the seashore without aim or energy from his fate and life, which had no purpose for earthly measurement. He realized that there was a death in his life. And he was a dead man for the new world. He felt as if he is at his funeral.

THE NIGHT OF THE KILLING OF THE PROSECUTOR

In Tbilisi, the national movement left its awful footprint. The capital city was turbulent and restless as if the whirlwind had overtaken it. In town was heard occasional gunshots from time to time. The streets were not lit by Illuminations anymore. From the house, windows were lit by flickering candles.

It was a frosty night of early spring.

The prosecutor Mirza Kurdiani was asleep in the armchair of his working room. He had not slept for the last three nights. The sound of the phone call woke him. Someone was persistently calling.

He felt heaviness in his eyelids from insomnia, barely opened his eyes and calmly answered it, "Hello, I am listening!"– but the other end was silent. Mirza returned to his work.

The only thing that was puzzling him was the problem of how to destroy and break down the so called Institute of Lawful Thieves. He was seeking ways on how could he get rid of this monster in the capital city. The situation made harder by corrupt policemen supporting this "Institute of Thieves' and, for this reason, it became too strong, like an undefeated castle.

Some of the police officers who were helping them were ruling it. And this power eventually became a monster, like an unguarded fortress. The castle of law and order was being destroyed from the inside. Mirza had to confront two great united forces.

The sound of the telephone ringing disturbed again his unpleasant thoughts. He answered. There still was silence at the other end.

Mirza stood up and went to the window. The city was in deep sleep. The rain was pouring turning to sleet and there were hungry dogs barking on the street. He cleared the window glass by hand and looked for a long time at the dark town. There was his lovely town as if it was dead.

Mirza Qurdiani was swimming in the vortex of criminals... and he was guessing how deeply he was sinking there. His only wish was to find out who were the traitors from law enforcement. Who sold his soul to the devil? He had some operative information and doubt was turning to certainty. He did not want to believe this terrible reality. The driver's occupation he canceled and he was driving his car himself, in this way he wanted to protect his guard. He did not want to sacrifice the staff serving him.

He was alone, opposite to the enemies of state.

The unambitious and dignified life of Mirza Kurdiani was granted the great authority over the whole system of prosecution.

Mirza was endlessly searching for a legitimate way to correctly respond to all messages. "The fish starts smelling from its head!" – This expression was like a rule in his life. If to information you do not respond properly, the offense cannot be solved. Therefore, it is necessary to look at the scene of the crime as soon as possible, and like that, in this way need to follow its hot clues. With professional honesty you need to collect signs or any different kind of evidence. It is better to get rid of the first offense, since it is possible to avoid the expected offenses, that can lead to the loss of human life and health. How can good police help the criminals? Of course, there are such betrayers or sellers, but fortunately the bad units there are only a few. Those with whom we need to fight loudly and to declare it loudly, blamed and isolated from the public. In this way can be avoided all negative consequences for the acceleration of crime. That can hurt society. Those whom we must fight loudly and strongly, and be ready for everlasting battle opposite them, it is not easy.

From his thoughts the prosecutor was roused by the phone ringing again. This time it was his family, he heard his wife's pleasant voice: "Are you still staying at work?"– Mirza promised to be home soon.

On the next day, newspapers broke the story:

On March 23, 1993, at 2 am, in Pekini Street in Tbilisi Mirza Qurdiani, the prosecutor, was killed at his flat entrance when he was getting out from his own car. An unknown young man approached him, who shot him with three bullets, two near to his heart and one in his head.

INVESTIGATOR OF PECULIAR CASES

It was terrible slushy weather. The city seemed to be in a deep sleep. The phone rang at three o'clock. It was an operative information officer. He informed Londa about the place of murder. The incident took place at the crossing of Pekini and Saburtalo Streets in Tbilisi. Was shot the prosecutor Mirza Qurdiani. The rest of the details would be found at the place of incident.

Londa had just arrived home. She looked in at her children, covered them with their blanket and kissed them on their forehead. Some fear took hold of her, the fear as if seeing her children for the last time. She had the same feelings at other times, but now the matter was very serious, the murder was concerning to her colleague, a person whose humanity and honesty was known to everyone.

Londa was captured by terrible thoughts. Murdering of Mirza Kurdiani was unimaginable, inconceivable.

The man who was considered as the dignified father of the jurisdiction, universal man, who almost never made mistakes. The man, who taught Londa and entire younger generations of jurisprudence. A lot of students were raised by him and delivered to protect the justice and welfare of our homeland. He has never cared about his glory or fame. He never thought about himself, his own life, just tried to increase the country's honest lawyers. Days and nights he was standing in defense of citizens in the capital city.

Londa was in shock. She called the elevator but soon she changed her decision and she chose to walk down from the fourth floor by the stairs. She was thinking about a thousand possible variations of this murderous event and instantly denied. It was too difficult to believe killing with three bullets in head and heart. And at last she took a decision, that definitely it was a hired killer, cold hearted murderer. The question was: was he either a military person, or an experienced policeman? – though she was thinking about this, but it was hard to believe.

She suddenly remembered that she was without her firearm and she had to get it from the General Prosecutor's Office.

Londa was driving from Ortachala to Saburtalo. She had an eight cylinder Mercedes and often had fuel problems. It was very difficult to get it. The civil war had not ended yet in the city. It was still going on. You could smell cordite in the air. She stopped at the petrol station, but they did not have any fuel. The petrol seller recognized her and offered to bring her petrol from the other petrol station in half an hour.

Londa had the opportunity to think again.

A coldness came over her. A deep and unpleasant feeling seized her. She still was thinking about the killing phenomenon. Londa had been working on murder cases for eight years and never had thought so deeply about this crime. There was only one opinion about killing, as this crime was an irreparable crime, as the dead could not be revived. She remembered the words of the great Russian writer Chekhov: "The shot is not a tragedy, tragedy is that, what happens before an end, before the shot is fired." You can help the wounded person, stolen things you can find, if your house will be burned, it can be restored, the events of trafficking criminals can return to society but the murdered person can never be given a second chance of life. Think about killing, murder the killer actually kills himself, because of, the prison walls never can make better your situation, if you are a killer.

Also as rules of Christianity teach us, the killed man goes without court to heaven, but killer never can get there. "Justice of Blood" so suitable this expression. It comes from the Georgian language. She felt proud. Perhaps, this name came from paying blood with blood, but name exactly express meaning of sense.

In the old times, when one person killed another, should be paid killers tribe with blood. It was an irreconcilable problem – the rule of taking blood for blood.

The murder is this case, in which the man is killed by man. You are killing the man and you are putting in grave danger all the members of his family forever.

What guilt can have a man, who does such things? What makes such a man to do it? Is it revenge? Self-interest? Cruelty? Financial?

What is it? An ordered murder?

Is it a killer that can kill ten men and more?

What a horrible thing can be murder in exchange for money, killing a person with self-esteem, a person who you don't know about, and did no cruel act for you. All your doing just for money.

We called such person a maniac

It is unbelievable, that the sum, taking or paid in this way, you must spend on saving your family and you cannot find other ways. And this is some devotion to your family, but if you just think in what way you earn this money, you will find an answer for it, that devoted person cannot commit such terrible crime against people he does not know, if he is normal.

There is left just one answer – it is coldblooded killer, and he can't be cured even in mental ways. What precise calculations do you need to study such a maniac?

At this time the question arises: which one is more guilty: the hired killer or the man who paid the killer?

The answer is one: the first is the mastermind of the murders and after the killer maniac, who with the reason of become rich, can take another person's life. And why himself is victim of subsequent maniac killer, who has been a victim of the enrichment and megalomania.

The investigator's thoughts battled with each other to beat possible mistakes and thus to find the truth.

What a pity it is that the modern criminality techniques have not been achieved for our country yet. The available technical means are unfortunately not developed, to find a killer and people ordering it.

The criminals often repeat the same crime. So the investigation should be conducted perfectly. Only one person's penalty cannot bring spring.

Londa was thinking about such modern cruel time and situations, full of resistance. She regretted that she had an active life in very bad time. It was a cruel time. Good friendships for people were lost due to lack of money. It was a shortage of fuel, so it was difficult to move around in the city. Only the criminals flashed in the city, people with guns were running in country and were taking from other people their last coins. So, the generation was ruined. The spirit was broken. The education was limited. The country turned out to be maelstrom vortex of criminals. This became the reason for the increase of murders and the orderings of murders.

Soon, car door was opened by the petrol seller with his hands full of petrol, in three-liter container. He was delighted that he could please the lady he respected.

Londa got out of her car to open the tank cap... So, she could move now.

Soon investigator Londa was at the scene of the murder.

VIEWING THE MURDER SCENE

In Tbilisi, in Saburtalo street a lot of people were gathered at the scene of the murder: local residents, operative workers and policemen with dogs. The victim, who was killed at his home entrance, was not able to get inside his house. The corpse was immediately moved to the prosthetic to conduct a forensic medical examination.

The studying the scene of killing took place in the open air for the reason that was dark night, with artificial lighting in wet rainy weather.

The murder site was located on the crossroads of Pekin and Saburtalo Streets. The car was standing near pedestrian walking on the Saburtalo street. The front tire was on the pedestrian footpath, and the rear wheels of the car in the corner of Pekin Street. It was the white colour of the Soviet origin car Volga124 with the state number 3213 GAA. The ignition key was in the on position. The left door was fully opened It seemed obvious that the key was placed in the ignition, or the car engine had stalled. Information dials showed 153538 km. After turning off the ignition, the experts began examining the background of the scene. On the outside of the vehicle there was not any sign of damage. Front of the car was found two spent bullets.

Afterwards, the experts took two kind of tests: a swab on a wet bacillus and one on a dry bacillus, which was carefully placed in evidence bags, which were dated and had the signatures of the participants. In the end, they were sealed with barcode in the special package. Mirza Kurdiani's car, after taking out his personal items, was sealed. Towards Investigator's actions from participating side in the surveillance no comments have been received.

The Prosecutor of the General Office of Georgia launched an investigation under Article 236 (12) of the Criminal Code of Georgia and Part 1 of Article 104 of the Criminal Code of Georgia, which meant using firearms. Intentional murder using aggravated assault in aggravating circumstances.

The investigative group was formed by Londa Amilakhvari. The group included three people, the three well known investigators: Gogita Zavradashvili, Dudu Arziani and Koka Saladze.

The investigation started at 23 March of 1993.

THE CASE HAS BEEN LAUNCHED, FIRST CLUE APPEARED

The investigation group were working day and night, learning every movement of the murdered man. But the murderers appeared to be well prepared. Suspicion was cast on legitimate thieves and some high-ranking police officers. The group found it difficult to open this case. The sixth month after the murder, its first clue appeared. Some reliable information entered to the prosecutor's office. Dudu arziani had been contacted by one person, who was among people at the night of murder and asked for a meeting. But this person was demanding that they would protect him. The telephone number was not registered there, nor whereabouts of the ringing place, which made suspicious of the real existence of the witness. The witness promised to come to them at 11 o'clock next morning, but he did not appear.

This situation made Londa worry.

Again, assembled members of the group and with help of special services to investigation to find out who was ringing them. The telephone number and location were not fixed. They talked for hours and hours about the situations.

Suddenly, the telephone rang again in Londa's office. She picked it up and the same time she switched to speaker. In the room, was the trembling voice of man, who was asking for a meeting personally with Londa without the attendees, just outside the building of the prosecutor's office. Londa suddenly agreed to a meeting.

The meeting was scheduled to take place in the café bar at the turtle lake, and which was opened only in the summer season. The person asking for the meeting, again demanded the police to protect him. The time was too short before the meeting. The guys were nervous. It was obvious, because the lake was functioning seasonally, and it was located on the edge of the forest, and there was a certain threat to this mysterious meeting in being alone.

The special service was preparing for the second morning of meetings. Londa could not meet with them, but on the phone she was warned not to show to the witness, her anxiety and fear. Londa was advised to wear white colored clothe to avoid them losing sight of her.

And so, it was decided to do the operation – "the meeting at turtle lake".

Thanks to God, in this investigative group were involved trust worthy, loyal fellow colleagues.

The operation was headed by general prosecutor of whole country general Jani Bibiluri.

In spite of this, Londa with feminine instinct had a fear, but all the time she was comforting herself that nothing would happened, but she remembered many incidents in this area and could not make herself calm. In such cases, she always remembered her father's suggestions that working on the prosecution was not a job for a woman, "god has given you the gift of writing, and why you are troubling yourself in the middle of the night?" – he was often saying her, but the same time he was encouraging her and called her "the courageous daughter of father" and if he had some secret, he always shared with her

Londa could not sleep all night. She weighed the pros and cons, thought over the nuances. She was thinking that the voice on the phone was familiar.

She had many times been afraid of death, but had overcome it. Only she could calm herself.

Suddenly, she planned something and called "Dudu Arziani" and asked him to take her to check the situation on the turtle lake. The same time she did not remember whereabouts of the cafe, where she planned to meet the stranger next day. Dudu advised her to go to bed and to rest, as next day could be very difficult. But Londa could not rest and decided to get in touch with her childhood friend, Nona. Nona was a juvenile inspector in Batumi and was in Tbilisi at the time on a training course.

Nona loved her and trusted her friend and did not turn her back on her. She went with Londa to check the location of the place of destination. In way for their security they let know about their plan to their coworker and warned him, if they would not appear at 5am, he could sound the alarm.

At three o'clock in the night, armed girls went to the lake. They found the hiding place, where they would not have been seen by anyone. The night was very dark. No lights were seen near the lake. Only the moonlight on the lake's shore showed tied up boat, that was shimmering like a drunken giant in the light. It was a nightmare. The girls were shocked to see this scene and just were dreaming about daylight. This would disappear their fear of darkness.

Suddenly, opposite the lake, they noticed a vehicle lights. The light slowly approached them. The girls were silently watching. The car stopped somewhere in about one hundred meters away and the breeze brought to then sounds of the men. They were guided by the light of the car. There were coming noises of two or three men. Then the men made control shot firing in the air. The breeze was bringing unclear words and some sending information to someone: "401, 401, can you hear us. No cars in this area, we cannot find any one". Then the light slowly moved away from Londa and Nona. The car was turning round. It's light slowly passed over the girls in their hiding place. The men were obviously looking for somebody. In the end the girls heard again, "No one is here. We are now going to the cafe in the woods."

With great caution and curiosity Londa opened her car door and got out to hear better what they were talking about, and what had happened. At the end, she was convinced that her intuition did not betray her. She realized, how dangerous the second day could be and once again she felt her superiority and said with menacing: "I am my father's brave girl and I will carry on doing my duty, I will break this case." It was very cold night and they were three hours without heater. Suddenly on the windscreen appeared drops of rain. "It started to thunder", – thought Londa and felt happy, as the sunder for her was a good sign.

Suddenly in radio they again heard: "We could not find them", and Londa recognized it. There, very near to the girl's whereabouts. It was her coworkers, Dudu Arziani and Koka Saladze, standing. Londa felt proud and happy, that she was not left without attention by her friends. She finally decided that she had reliable friends. After that night she always trusted them.

Soon the men left that area, they could not find the girls.

That night's secret visit to the turtle lake was forever left between Londa and Nona.

ON TURTLE LAKE

September 10, 1993 was the day of meeting with the witness of the murder.

The ringing of the alarm woke Londa. It was 10 o'clock. The weather was fine with the grace of god. The sun loosed itself from the captivity of clouds and was sneaking into the room. The sun light was feeding sleepless Londa's soul and tired body. She got up from her bed and headed to the mirror, it was wide, massive and carved and it was as a sacred thing for Londa.

The mirror was always objective and straightforward to her, more than any of her friends. Londa would be 33 years old in February. It is the age of Christ, and she thought it was the age of being ready to meet with Christian morality with gracious pride. Maria was dividing human life in to two parts: first part was the age up to 33, and another after 33. Exactly to the age of 33, people will pass all the tests of life. Sometimes, it seems that in front of you has opened a huge and wide abyss, and you think that, it is waiting for you with silence pleasure to slip into it, as if it is ready to swallow you. All dignities of person form at this age. You are looking for true values of life. It is important to lift weaker people up by making positive comments about them. If you make them believe, one trusts them, however, if you assume that their fate is in their own hands, they will change immediately, will discover strengths, to stand strongly and firmly on their own feet. Unrealized excitement captured Londa, when she was imagining that she could help her coworkers to get relieve from their burdens and did this with pleasure. As if mirror had woken her up. On her face could be seen traces of previous day's worrying. Londa felt a sense of shame in her heart for the absurd fear she had gone through. She already had some grey hair and this was not genetic. Each of her grey hairs had its own painful history. Her eyes were also very sorrowful, with unexplained melancholy. The reason of this sadness was her profession, full of worries and painful mysteries. She couldn't share it with anyone, not friends and nor with her family. Yes, this occupation was self-destructive monster, the reason for living in the hidden reality.

Londas's colleagues arrived and from outside they gave a signal to her, that they were waiting outside. In accordance with the agreement, she should wear light coloured clothes. She was dressed in tobacco coloured dress, which was very smart. She took with her a pen, the protocol form, the appropriate legal literature in her bag and left her flat. The colleagues were worried, all felt anxious. They did not want to make any mistakes. The fate of many people were at risk.

Was there a real person, who could really help them, or was it a trap?

The truth will out and hopefully will not be lost. Colleagues were silent on their way. Everyone was thinking about the final it could be a long disappointment, or could be a breakthrough in their investigation.

Londa looked at Dudu and remembered adventure of the previous night.

"I know exactly where a café bar is. In the day times their people walk, taking exercise. There won't be any threat to anyone. There, hopefully. Although, anyway we're mobilized!" said Dudu, when they arrived at the Turtle Lake. Londa knew the whereabouts of the café bar and she asked the driver to go to the right. Gogita Zavradashvili, who was driving the car, and was a very serious and earnest man, – astonishingly asked her, wherefrom she knew this cafe bar, as it was just yesterday, she said she did not remember it. The men looked at each other and then looked at Londa suspiciously. They knew the character of Londa, as she could have gone alone in that vulnerable place. Londa did not answer, as she left her secret for later.

The car approached to the cafe bar and Londa got out from the car and continued walking alone. It was very quiet there. No people were near there, just a couple of ducks were swimming on the lake. The sun was hiding behind foggy clouds and around it seemed mysterious.

It was 2 o'clock, the arranged time. The building, where the café bar was located, seemed to have been left without attention. The entrance doors were closed and nailed. The many panes of glass were broken. At the entrance, there were several cartridge cases.

It gave the impression of a completely desolate place.

Londa waited for an hour, nobody came. Then Londa gave a signal to her colleagues as arranged time for meeting had expired. The men came out from their hiding places and joined Londa. They could not decide what to do next, hesitating. But after decided to fire a shot in the air as they did not like this silence. Dudu made a shot in air and waited for the result. No result. Just still silence.

They did not like this silence. There was no movement from the building or a sign of life. This invitation looked as a trap or a hoax.

For almost two days, they observed the café bar, but no one appeared there. No one ever entered or left its door.

Was it just a dirty game, or the intention to attack the operative service?

Londa thought long enough and then decided that the operation of September 10th should be delayed for several days, and observation of the location spot should be continued by special services.

Koka could not wait and broke with his foot the nailed door. In the small hall they found everything disturbed. Londa asked her two coworkers to stay outside. Koka and Londa entered inside. Londa's attention was taken by large amount of rubbish, dirty plates and glasses and lots of other kinds of things, among them, there on the table was an empty "Pshenichnaia'Wodka bottle. There were also two unspent bullets in the floor.

Koka entered another room. Londa took the gloves out of her bag and put them on. The bullets were carefully removed, and the light cups were placed in plastic bug and continued to explore the hall.

Londa could not hear any noise of Koka's movement. She tried to enter another room, where Koka went, but she could not do, as it was absolutely dark. Londa ran out and let the others know about Koka's disappearance. Everyone was in shock. They requested supporting group for help. A message came through not to enter that room, were Koka disappeared and not to perform any action until they arrived. In about 40minutes the supporting team arrived. Several operative cars were added. They were armed and invaded the building. The second room, where Koka disappeared, did not have any windows. The room was in darkness. They were full of astonishment, were looking for Koka and calling him. It seemed like magic. Then they suddenly heard an unusual squeak, and Goga went to the same side of room with its torch in his hand where the sound was heard and saw a huge trench from where started a tunnel. Koka was lying in the trench unconscious. He was taken up with great care.

Londa was stunned. She now was thinking of the tunnel that was the hiding place for the criminal world. It was a new clue for investigation. She wondered, if who was the caller. The first version was that it was a person who really knew the details of the murder, second version: somebody knew about the hiding place of the criminal lair and informed police to find out about it, and third: it was calling the killer himself and played with the police and was informing them about a vital building. But one great thing was done that they found out a serious clue, a very interesting thing.

BALLISTIC EXPERTISE

The situation in which the investigative group found itself, was so unique that, not even a scriptwriter could create an analogy of it.

Londa had to solve a new puzzle now. The old case was not finished yet and added a new one. It was horrible to think about, that the murderer walks in the city, and he possible takes a seat next to you on the bus, or he can ask you to light his cigarette in the street and you do not know who he is, and the same thing can happen with the phone calls: he has the advantage, as he knows who you are.

Londa felt in a difficult position, for the first time she realized that she was not able to defend herself and professional dignity just with her uniform and rank; it was necessary to get new equipment, and new information that would move the investigation forward.

Londa waited for three days for her bosses' attention, as they were very busy. She was tense and afraid that she did not want anyone to interfere roughly with the tunnel operation. She still believed that all details would be learned with cautions. Londa, for some reason, could not believe that the man who was summoned to turtle lake that day, was not a witness but could be a murderer. She took out the sealed pack and decided to legalize it by register it with the court and then to arrange a ballistic examination.

Londa generally could not bear making a professional mistake. Though she always asked her colleagues for advice. She remembered her first steps in the supreme court. For three days a prosecutor of great experience, Emzar Tkesheladze, was helping her. One of the hardest cases was a review in the supreme court. The case was really unprecedented; a mother was accused in killing her own son. Londa did not want to believe it. The sorrow attacked her. It was the big mistake to involve a beginner prosecutor in such a heavy case, but she knew her life never had been easy, she had to work with huge problems herself to get good results. The big mistake was the involvement of the new prosecutor in such a difficult case, but she was used to working alone on difficult problems. It was not easy for her to have the greatest problems to fight alone and to fight until the desired results. But Londa realized that this case about mother and son could not be finished easily. The elder colleague Emzar Tkesheladze, who gave her good advice, said before the court proceedings:

"What do you think, can I defeat you in this particular case? – I've learned about ten thousand cases and now if you ask to me how I decided this case, I can't answer to you about it. Everything is as individual as a person. It is easily possible that about this case in three days you will know more than me. Just the procedures I cannot be mistaken. That is why we, prosecutors, meet every Friday in charge of the management of accusation prosecutors and such heavy decisions arrange together. But I still advise you, as your friend, to work in your inner belief and wait for the time that will work on you and experience you. Remember that behind of every offender is their family and this family is the most damaging one. So you should be absolutely objective, the decision what you need to make, never let the others to decide or to resolve it. It's just my advice to consult with your colleagues, it's not a shame, but shame is to punish an innocent person". Londa returned the "Mother and son's case" to the previous investigation and later it turned out that senior colleagues were also in the same opinion about this particular case.

But Londa most trusted Temur Manavidze, the Chief Prosecutor of Georgia, because he had great experience and was very reasonable, sensible and prudent person. If the accuser does not have an internal censor or conscience, he or she will damage themselves and others too.

Londa made the decision after so much thinking, to arrange a ballistic and tactical examination for the purpose of examining prints on bullets and "Vodka" glasses.

She heard cautious knocking on the door. Londa invited the caller in. The door opened and Koka stepped in. He asked respectfully whether he disturbed her with his entering her room.

Londa felt uncomfortable, as if she had been caught in stealing and owner was now talking to her: "What are we going to do? When can we continue working in tunnel? It is the most dangerous and threatening area in this case. First of all, you need to find out who's the caller? Secondly, it is necessary to buy the phone, which can save numbers, and third: need to do searching works in the café bar, all the items that exist there need to be taken and examined. Londa told him, that she found in café bar lots of things and put them in an evidence bag, decided to open her secret to Koka. Koka listened to Londa and praised her:

"It is very clever of you. You gathered all evidence. It is possible, that tomorrow, when we arrive at the tunnel there won't be anything. These things could help us. If the killer was the author of the call, then, he would not let us have those bullets on a plate. But if he is the witness of the killing, he is ready to open our ways. He is sincere".

Londa asked thoughtfully: "So, why he did hide and why he did not warn us about possible dangers? It was definitely a criminal lair. Perhaps he knew that on September 10th, there, in café would not be any criminals. We made everything with great cautious in tunnel, before we left it. There was not left even our traces". She slowly one by one, show him her procured things, which were sealed and signed. Koka was overwhelmed by hearing this news. He did not attend the searching process with clear reason.

TURTLE LAKE – CAFE BAR

On the night before the search, Londa mobilized her mind. Remembered one of Mirza Kurdiani's lectures in criminal proceedings.

Mirza Kurdiani was one of the most powerful professors. In his lessons there always was dead silence. Mirza never would give to his student unmerited censure, but his remark always was polite and comprehensive.

No normal student could dare to get irresponsible in his lessons. It is a bad comparison, but the blind is known by two factors: the first is how to move, steps taken, with knocking walking stick; the second, it feels the light, on which side it is. So had learned about Mr. Mirza, each of his student's potential capabilities.

He was asking his students the questions as far as they were able to answer them. He knew all their possibilities. His attitude to his students was as much as pure as the water in the glass test-tube. The main thing was that from one hundred students, he felt each of their character and later he accordingly evaluated them. He imposed that there should not be written highest mark, as jurisprudence is not a perfect science and therefore can never be targeting, the criminal matter how the outcome ends. Because of this, Mirza claimed that since the results cannot be focused on the maximum rate it should not be estimated – nor students and not even cases.

Londa, from sadness, became restless. She did not remember her personal activities as she was so strongly touched by every criminal case, but nothing was comparable to Mirza Qurdiani's murder.

The murdering of the Qurdiani was not a normal, usual story. This was the result of battle of between two great societies. Of course, until there is humanity, there will be eternal and endless battle between two societies, – between the crimes and justice, and this battle will be sometimes civilized and sometimes combative.

And even the hands of the jurisdiction of justice, this relationship also has its own laws, explanation; its own rail track, railway.

If the train becomes derailed, the passengers become predestined.

Yes, it is true. And if one side the betrayer enters, immediately between these two forces legal relationship is terminated and a new individual plans to build a relationship is formed, raised the unwritten laws, which gives rise to corruption and break down of good and just laws.

And this time, only scientific knowledge and practice procedures do not help the case. The fate of the case depends on the whole experience of the investigator.

At the same time, what kind of caution is necessary to prevent innocent people from getting into the bill? In this situation, he becomes, the so called, the accused but you are the sinner. Because, in this case, just professional instinct and feeling are not enough, it is necessary a personal decency and a calmness of the soul. The investigator should not listen to the advice of other people, because an accused innocent person will one day be free, but sinner prosecutor will remain with his sin forever. It is said: every real man need to have two names: one stays here, in this world, and another follows him to the next world.

In our particular case, Mirza Qurdiani had both names stainless and unsullied.

Mr. Mirza had never abrogated breaking the rules of life, but his killer lost everything and sold his soul to the devil! It is so cruel, when the human being takes life from another human being the most precious thing, everyone has, what is given from god. This time you are selling your own soul to devil. This is ignorance of the moral laws – and again, she remembered the words of Emmanuel Kant: act as that your behavior would become as standard norm of a universal legislation."

Londa had no right to make a mistake. She knew that truth was one that would never have lost its significance. And the truth and righteousness, of course, would lead her to the temple.

Londa's investigative group was preparing for a planned search of the café bar at the Turtle Lake. The search should be conducted in full compliance with the criminal procedure rules. The participants of the search were assembled and consulted. Before starting searching they observed the searching place. They searched also where the tunnel lead. They mended the door of tunnel and after officially sealed it. And was set up twenty-four-hour observation.

The situation was controlled by a special purpose service. The search was conducted in full compliance with criminal procedural norms. Investigative action was carried out in a peaceful situation and within the law. During this time of search they discovered illegal things, among them weapons and bullets. They were packaged up after counting. There was a disc found that was also sealed by the signature confirmed and acknowledged and was added to the case. What concerns two bullets, removed by Londa, on their first visit, and two drinking glasses due to urgent necessity the court had examined and legalized it because, delaying it could course problems for investigation. Logged cases of recovered items. The court found that delay could result in the destruction of the actual data for the investigation.

AN ANONYMOUS LETTER TO THE PROSECUTOR 30TH SEPTEMBER, 1993.

"Ms. Londa, I am the person, who treats the truth fairly and politely, because I believe that the truth never loses its meaning. Despite the delays in investigation, I know that the truth will be established and celebrated.

On the march 23, 1993, I saw how Mirza Kurdiani was killed. I live close to the place of the incident. The young man, about 2527 years old, that was armed with a pistol, fired at the prosecutor. He was standing about three meters away from Mirza Qurdiani and killed him with 3 bullets. I don't know that person. I have not seen him before. But because I was close to the killer, I got a good look at him: he was dressed in a tobacco-colored coat, wearing a black knitted hat, baton-style "batiks". He was a slim man, and his height would be about 1 m 85 cm. He had a long face and a straight nose. When I saw him, it was the moment he fired. He also saw me that I was watching but he did not give me any attention. I survived, as he did not express any aggression towards me, and he fled instantly. He was alone. I knew the deceased prosecutor, because he lived in my district. I was not able to tell you about this matter, as I felt unprotected and I am not sure if the killer knows me or not. It is possible, that the killer knows me.

In this letter, an absolute truth is described. You can look for the murderer by this data. If my information helps you to detain him, I will come to identify him. If you create a photo fit, please show on the television.

With respect a neighbor of Mirza Kurdiani.

THINKING ABOUT THE FATE OF MAIN WITNESS

Londa read the anonymous letter several times. The facts in it were logical. The main matter, the investigation was interested in, was the connection between the letter and the items and things, discovered after the searching the café bar in turtle lake area. Some connection was clearly between the author of the letter and the anonymous phone call. The witness was not intimidated, but looked rather concerned. The reason for his fear was obvious. In reality, appearing openly, could be dangerous, for the witness because, the killer was unknown to the witness. The killer was quiet and calm, because six months after the incident the investigation was practically silent. If there appeared one more witness of the incident, the trial could have been based on the information contained in the letter. The author of the anonymous letter was difficult to find. For that reason, from the letter could be seen that he was from neighborhood of Mirza Kurdiani. Perhaps the killer also was the neighbor of Mirza Qurdiani? – but if we consider the fact that the letter holder did not recognize the killer, then it will be logical if we think that the murderer is from a different area.

Londa ruminated about the facts of neighbors of Mirza Kurdiani. It was a long time from the initial questioning of his neighbors. All of them gave the same testimony, that they could not see who killed him, only heard the sound of three shots. It was necessary to do more work with them. It is clear that there are some people, who have seen the murder but feel unsafe. And if a witness is there in reality, it is fully possible, that he or she has the family and they were notified about it too. Of course they would say that, because of the great emotions, that they witnessed a terrible and disgusting murder. It is possible too, that the killer found out himself about the letter writer and warned him or frightened him. He saw the witness face to face. He could remember his face. It is possible too, that he was watching that person until he did not determine who the person was and where he lived. We know that the high ranking officials were fighting against Mirza Qurdiani and they would not have any problems to organize an operation to find the witness, to identify the person who witnessed this murder.

It is possible too, that the murdered man could had been watched by murderers and they could had seen the witness themselves too. And if they know about him, he will be totally exposed, and his family members at the same time. It is possible too, that the witness has not been seen.

The witness does not know, who the killer is, he only visually can describe him.

Londa was thinking endlessly of how real was the anonymous person, described in the letter. She also thought that the anonymous letter could be sent by the criminals. Maybe the murderer is not 25 years old, but a 50 years old, or as it figures in the letter is not high and thin, rather it is short and fat and nose has not precise and accurate, how was written in the letter.

Then what meaning can have the creation of the photo fit? What is the significance of it? It is obviously a lack of information. It is bad too, that there, in the place of the murder area video surveillance cameras were not fixed. In this case, the main focus must be given to the killing weapon. The need to find it. However, how it will be possible to find it unless this weapon is used to commit a new crime. The case obviously is very complicated. Investigation is thoroughly studying enemies around Mirza Kurdiani. We are dealing with a well-rounded circle. Probably the members of the investigative croup will demand soon to be protected. Great caution will be needed in getting each piece of information.

SPECIAL MEETING

Londa planned a special meeting for October 2nd. The members of the investigative group were on duty all the previous night and so they were very tired, but all of them arrived on time. The reason for the meeting was an anonymous letter.

The author of the letter looked quite intellectual, with great experience of life and human dignity. Londa had difficulty thinking negatively because the killer could not write such sincere words. It was a witness, but how could she establish facts about his identity? The letter was not rewritten, because one of the words had been crossed. When you are thinking and looking for a substitute, you find it and change, but you cross out an old one. While Londa was in deep thoughts, all her colleagues were gathered around her, worrying, with smoking cigarettes in their hands.

The meeting started in a silence, everybody was quiet for about five minutes. After Londa said:

As we see, we are facing a serious obstacle. It will be our only chance to work on what evidence we have. If something is there helpful for our investigation, we will continue working on this case. The only thing that we can hold, is that the witness lives close to Mirza Kurdiani. This is a thoughtful phrase. The living near him doesn't mean to be his floor neighbor, nor of being an inhabitant of the same block, where lived Mirza Qurdiani. It is possible he was going to the other house and in his way accidentally faced this murderer. What are we doing to establish it? We cannot put our hands to our breast and wait.

Suddenly, Koka said, "I checked the number of blocks around mirza. There are five residential buildings and in each building contains from 70 to 100 families."

Dudu interrupted, "I have this idea about the person x. If he was returning from his work place to home at 2 at night, it is obvious, that he was returning passing Qurdiani's block, or through block, if he lives behind mirza's block, there is one five story house. Because there is a narrow way which goes from mirza's building and there is lighting and maybe this is the way he had chosen."

Koka reminded him that mirza lived in the second entrance.

So, needed to think that he was going either the first entrance or in the back way to the five store building.

Maria had a new thoughts and added: "The number of people who could be questioned, reduced, and if we imagine that x was standing face to face to the murderer, it seems that witness is either from mirza's entrance, or it is easily possible, if he is from five store building behind that block of flats. The third option is more acceptable because there is a five store building."

The discussion lasted for a long time, and finally came to a conclusion that to discover the killer needed to create a photo fit, otherwise they had no chance of getting a description of killer.

The letter was reread again... And they discovered two more important moments. One, that x person was coming back from the night shift, it worked and could be arrange observing around 2 at night. If he still works in the same place, he should go back home at night at about 2 o'clock. The observation should last longer, about 10 days, because the shift can be done once in three days. And if they have found that the same person has come at the same time twice, then they will achieve the results they were expecting.

At the meeting Koka and Dudu were ordered to learn the names of the inhabitants of the residential buildings and study their activities in general. With this it would be possible to find out the above facts that the witness worked as a shift engineer in the shoe factory...

"Why an engineer and not a worker?" asked Dudu.

Londa immediately reminded him about the contents of the letter and noted that the writer of this letter must be well educated. Colleges received their assignments and were dismissed.

LONDA'S THOUGHTS

On the 18th of October, the General Prosecutor of Georgia satisfied the requirements of Londa Amilakhvari and handed her expensive mobile phones for all members of the investigative group for easy communications. Now the members of the group will not have trouble contacting each other.

Londa's thoughts were related to Mirza Kurdiani's residential building. Did the witness really lived in the entrance of the mirza or he lived in the first entrance. Did he know mirza Kurdiani's family members? Or, it is unbelievable that the witness of the murder did not attend the burial of mirza. However, mirza Kurdiani's funeral was almost all employees of the prosecutor's office, including Londa. Perhaps the witness had a message from the murderers and they forbid him to attend the victim's funeral.

Londa called Dudu and asked him to take care of the planned operation. He had a private assignment to go to the shoe factory and ask them, if was there working or not someone from Pekin street, numbered 8 or 9, from their staff. And in the positive case who was it, an ordinary employee or manager.

In the factory were working 800 people. The staff service was served by 8 employees. The accounting was alphabetical.

Dudu decided to question the head of the factory. He warned him, to keep this request secretly. The Head of Staff, David ChikoVani took into consideration the request of the investigation, calling each employee of the staff service and asked them to bring list of employees and their addresses and photos.

Serious work was done in the shoe factory and the results were achieved. It turned out that in the 8th number of Pekin street really lived the head of the shoe factory shift, Solomon Kalandadze. Investigation requested the personal case of the person, included his photo.

What a happy morning it was for Londa. After a long time, they finally got to the main witness. The personal case of the witness was studied, obviously, he was no longer the x person. Now, the investigator was aware of who was the witness of the murder and what kind of person he was.

The investigative group had a new puzzle now. How to bring the witness, Soloman Kalandadze, to the office? Londa remembered her late colleague Mirza Qurdiani's caution. He sacrificed himself but did not put his driver or security guard at risk. They were only dismissed for the fact that they were in at the danger of being overwhelmed. Even now, there was a similar scene, a witness could be killed for witnessing the scene of the murder. Because the murderer was standing in front of him. Solomon Kalandadze naturally obviously saw how was killed Mirza Kurdiani. Londa thought that she had to think carefully in order to conduct an investigation that would not harm Solomon. Therefore, the relevant services were given special assignments to witness Kalandadze, who had been wary of the murder suspect, was absolutely safe.

REPORT TO THE GENERAL PROSECUTOR OF GEORGIA TO ESTABLISH A WITNESS

On October 20th, Londa was consulted with her colleagues. It was not an ordinary consultation. Now, they had a good clue to follow, and it demanded very accurate, pedantic, and right method of approach.

This time Londa arranged a meeting for the reason that she had decided to withdraw her candidature to hand it over to a more experienced investigator. Hearing it disappointed her colleagues. They were surprised. They unanimously stated that Londa was more focused, organized and observed, than any of them. Somehow the group members were deeply moved by Londa's phenomenon. After this statement it was clear that all of them were more concerned about Londa's statement. It was unimaginable Londa's resigning from leadership. Dudu loudly expressed his opinion about female colleagues:

In my opinion, there is no profession, where the role of men and women must be isolated from each other. It's time to adapt to the idea that women are more organized than men. These are women's simple advantage, not their inherent quality.

The men liked Dudu's speech and loudly gave an "oath" never to discuss such issue.

Londa once again felt the advantage and continued to speak her speech with double power.

Soon there was phone call: Eka Kakauridze, secretary of the prosecutor general's office, inform them, that the prosecutor of general office was inviting Londa and her group for consultation.

This information troubled the young people and before the main consultation they reviewed once again the information collected by them.

The meeting lasted for 2 hours, and it was attended by Varlam Macharashvili, Head of Criminal Service and otar beraia, head of investigation unit.

Investigators of particularly important cases reported to the general of justice, one by one about their statements about the investigative actions carried out on the witness's personality and occupation. The investigation still was continuing. Witness Solomon Kalandadze should be questioned urgently. It was necessary to take special measures to protect him physically. It should have been started by operative officers to ensure that Kalandadze was safe, in order if he was being constantly checked by criminals. What he was dealing with and who he was in contact with? Had he been threatened? It was decided that the witness had to be questioned not in the premises of the prosecutor's office. The general prosecutor requested Londa Amilakhvari for further action plan and thanked her for the work carried out by her group.

MIRACULOUS SPANIEL

While Londa had been waiting for the expert's conclusion, she drifted into deep thoughts:

Should the witness be questioned first or should they wait for the expert's results? No one can teach or tell you how to behave, if you don't know yourself. Londa was considering both issues and gave preference to Solomon Kalandadze's interrogation.

Instead of one Londa found several pictures of Solomon kalandadze and was looking at them on her table. Could it be the person, with whom they are hoping so much of, or are they being led on a wild goose chase.

Londa set out the questions she had to put to the witness. The investigation knew that this person had a wonderful family. His wife was Kipshidze clinic's well-known cardiologist, Lali Berikishvili. They had a son, Saba, who was a student of Tbilisi State University and had a French breed black bulldog in his family, which all members of the family took turns walking.

Londa suddenly came to think that she first should check the information and get acquainted with Solomon Kalandadze's family members. According to the reported information, the kalandadze had a dog. Every morning and evening, Mrs. Lali was taking the dog walking at 89 am, and later at 9 pm, sometimes Solomon and Jaba took it.

On 30th of October Londa woke up with anxiety. She was late for Pekin street. She should have to pass her friend, Lile Dzidziguri, on Bulachauri street and should take her dog "springer spaniel" for a walk.

She was little bit afraid of this dog, because had not seen it in the last two weeks, and it was possible, that the dog would not want to go with her. But when she arrived, she made a fuss of the dog. Soon they were on their way. Londa left her car at the entrance of Lile's house and crossed the Saburtalo street with the dog. Just after, later, she noticed that dog was without a muzzle. She had been bitten on her hands and feet when she was a child, because she was afraid of dogs.

Londa noticed a nice woman dressed in a sporty dress. She approached her and sat nearby seat. But this woman did not have a dog, as Londa guessed, she was training. "Spaniel" started playing with her... Running around. The woman stopped and caressed the dog. "spaniel" started wagging and laying at her feet on the ground. The stranger left her training and continued playing with the dog. Londa grabbed her chance and moved closer to them.

"What is your dog called?" the woman asked her.

"Gucci," Londa answered without delay.

"There are four dogs in our building, but none of them have such a good nature," the woman continued caressing the dog.

"I live on Bulachauri, so many dogs gather in the yard there and then fight, so I chose to bring her here," said Londa.

"You are lucky today. Three or four dogs gather here in the mornings. Sometimes they fight with each other and this time do not care about each other, their owners cannot stop them."

"I agree with you. It was evening, about 8 pm. I was walking with my dog. A man walked out with the black bulldog puppy, and suddenly attacked my "Gucci". If not for the help of that courageous dog owner, I would not know what to do. He separated them."

"I remember. I know the owner of the bulldog. He is known as Solomon and he's very fond of the dog. Almost every day three member of his family take their bulldog for walks."

"People who do not love dogs, I do not think that they are human beings," continued Londa.

"Yes, I agree with you. He has got a wonderful family. His wife is a doctor. Especially Mrs. Lali loves "Chichi", you probably understood, "Chichi" is the bulldog's name."

"And Solomon is a doctor, too?" asked Londa.

"No, Mr. Solomon has been working in the shoe factory for years."

"There is still a shoe factory?" Londa asked.

"Yes, fortunately, this factory is all we have left. During the war, I know from Solomon that they were sending extra warm fabrics to Sokhumi for Georgian soldiers."

"I'm really surprised. No factories are working in Tbilisi. Everything is for sale, " Londa could not stop herself.

"Mr. Solomon contributed to the rescue of this factory. It is really surprising that there is so much extortion, but it did not stop working even for a day."

Londa looked at her with astonishment. The woman came to understand the reason of surprise and continued:

Yes, as I know from Mrs. Lali. I often say that criminals have been sabotaging him, but Solomon has not stopped even for one day, he doesn't care about his wellbeing, he does not have even his own car and he from his night shift often comes walking from "Isani". It is so far away. They are my door neighbours, and when I hear the noise of Kalandadze's door at night, I know it is about 2 am.

"Do you live in this house?" asked Londa.

No, I live behind this building.

Well, I remember, what terrible murder happened here... The murder of the prosecutor, you probably know... About seven months ago.

Yes, I do... I know well the family of Mirza Kurdiani... Are there still in Georgia investigations? – So famous man was shot dead in the center of the city and the killer is still unknown.

"What can I call you?" asked Londa.

I'm Rusudan... Rusudan Miqaya.

Ms. Rusudan, perhaps you know, was there any one, who could see this incident. Hard to believe that in this area, surrounded with so many houses, no one saw it. Maybe someone had witnessed this murder?

No, my girl, I know that no one saw it... If was so, someone would say it among neighbors.

I am a chair of this community and I often, when people need my help, when it is a laugh or in sadness, I am collecting money, but never heard anything, no one said nothing. Just one thing is worrying me. On the ill-fated night, when mirza Kurdiani's life was thrown out by the robbers, I heard the sound of gun fire, twice or three times. To tell the truth, there is a sound of shooting here, often happens and because of a situation of war no one is surprised. How could I imagine that shots were for Mirza, the same time from my window cannot see their entrance, where he was killed.

Did it happen in the entrance?

No, as I know from neighbors, he was shot before entering the entrance.

"And neighbors do not know anything either?" asked Londa.

What can I say, my girl, people are afraid, can't you see it, what time is it? The prosecutor was killed in the middle of center of the city and who will spare us? But is there one suspicious, that never gives me peace, – said Ms. Rusudan.

What the factor you talk about? – asked Londa.

I don't know but I know that I never can say it to investigation. But from the gun fire, in 510 minutes I heard the footsteps at Kalandadze's door. Though I knew that Solomon Kalandadze was coming back from the night shift.

Yes, but you said that it would be 2 am and the night shift is usually change after 12 hours.

No, I want to tell you, that I worked with Solomon for a short time in his factory as a Business Analyst and I know their inner world. It happened after 12 o'clock. At that time there was no transport, and as I have already said, as Solomon did not have a car, he often walked. That night I know exactly that it would be 2 am he came home.

Poor man... It would be in fear, and it is possible, he witnessed that terrible murder too. I can imagine his feeling.

"I know that he witnessed this murder, but it is possible,

he did not notice from where shots were fired," continued Rusudan.

"I learned the next morning that there was a man standing near the killer who saw how the prosecutor was shot," Londa said.

Solomon never talks about it. The next morning, his wife said that they were lucky that killer did not kill her husband too. It is not worth talking about this issue now. Solomon and his family were definitely seriously afraid. After the accident as gets darker they are at home. One thing I know is that Solomon was released from night shifts and is at home at 6 o'clock in the evening. They locked themselves in too. Hardly to open doors to anyone. If I do not accidentally meet them in the entrance or street, they don't contact me.

Well, but you say that they are walking a dog?

O, good, you reminded me, do they keep still their dog on the balcony, I want to see it?

Londa followed her with her "spaniel".

Rusudan looked at the top the block and show her "bulldog" on the 2nd floor balcony. Above, the bulldog suddenly saw the "spaniel" and started barking at her. "spaniel" was also barking from the courtyard. In the meantime, Mrs. Lali appeared on the balcony:

Rusa, please, take your dog, otherwise "Chichi" will wake the neighbors.

Rusudan sincerely offered Mrs. Lali to take "Chichi" for a walk. Lali answered, that her husband's duty was it for the next morning and he would take it out. Lali thanked the neighbor. Londa looked at her watch. The time had run fast.

She changed with Rusudan her phone number, promised friendship to her and said goodbye. After that, she held it in her hands and took it to Lile, his owner, her miraculous "spaniel".

BLACK "BULLDOG"

The second morning Londa took for a walk again Lile's "spaniel". She had a hope that she would meet the Kalandadze, walking with his white hearten 'bulldog' as she was expecting. Londa was excited, it seemed that dog felt it also. She was running around Londa and demanded from her more and more caressing. Unexpectedly, "Gucci" began grumbling and sniffing and went in deeper to bushes, his courage and fear had been chasing each other. The dog started barking. Londa could not stop 'Gucci', she attacked the black bulldog. Soon appeared the dog owner, the man in his middle ages. He interfered between dogs calling his dog:

Chichi, what are you doing? – And he demanded from his dog to lie on the ground. The dog stopped and obeyed his order: he lay on the ground.

Londa expressed gratitude to the man and added:

"If you did not interfere, it would end up badly. Do you live here?" asked the man.

No, it's a friend's dog, she did not have any time and I decided to walk it.

"Does she live near here?" asked the man. "Yes, on Shartava street."

"Now, I remembered that a week ago, I saw this dog in shop," Nikora said the man.

Perhaps it would be this dog, because the owner lives there.

"What can I call you?" asked the man.

Londa... And, what should I call you?

I'm Solomon, Soliko, I live here in the back yard. Suddenly, came noise of gunfire.

"What's going on?" Londa was scared.

"Do not worry. Why are you surprised? In this yard, a few months ago, a horrible murder occurred," said Solomon.

"What murder?" asked Londa.

You might hear from television, a high profile prosecutor was killed, a very good man.

Who, the prosecutor?

Have not you really heard, I cannot believe it, – Solomon said with a feeling of pity.

O, I remember now... The prosecutor's office could not find anything about the killer, – said Londa. – it will not go unsolved, because as I know someone saw this incident, what a heart should endure and not tell the truth. – she continued.

Oh, my girl, if it was so easy to tell the truth, would not be it problem. Did not you hear five minutes go machine gun that was fired? The city is in the hands of criminals, but if the witness is slightly protected, nothing will stop it, such wonderful man was killed by the outsiders.

Is witness known?

There must be some witness, but the main problem is that there is not protection mechanism for such people.

"Is it possible, that the murderers intimidated witnesses?" she asked.

I think so that the witness is intimidated. – Solomon spoke slowly.

"The witness has a family, perhaps they are also defenseless," said Londa.

No, they were probably warned by killers.

"In this murder, this case cannot really be reopened. Maybe this family is being watched permanently not to meet any one and not to spread some information," said Londa in the low tone, stood up and called "Gucci ".

Londa noticed that two men stood at the lighthouse and were spying in the entrance. They did not wear seasonal clothes. On top of the "captions", they both have black sunglasses. Londa realized that Solomon really was watched. However, neither Londa dressed in seasonal clothes. She was in sports form. On top of her head was wearing a sports cap. The hair was folded in a hat, which obviously changed her image and age.

Londa apologized to him and called "Gucci" again.

"Gucci" played with a black bulldog. Solomon asked to exchange Londa telephone numbers, removed the pen from his heart pocket and wrote his number.

Londa wrote to Solomon Lile's home number.

But, for two or three months we perhaps leave the town, the whole family... At the end of the month we will go. If I get your call until then I will invite you my home and acquaint with my family...– and after again with the joke Solomon continued: my white hearten "Chichi" acquainted me a lot of nice people.

Then he said bye-bye happily to Londa and gave her the pen as sign of their friendship.

NEW THOUGHT

Londa could not sleep the whole night. A new worry appeared for her, she realized that it was a mistake to meet this person. Because in her own eyes she saw two men in black glasses standing in the entrance, with "hoodies" pooled over and seemed to be watching at the actions of Solomon.

Of course, Solomon is an ordinary citizen and did not even notice the two strangers spying on him. If General Rule: Mirza Kurdiani was killed by big boss, it could not be excluded the boys were sent by the murderer as watchers to check all the movements of the isolated Kalandadze. It seemed that all the steps taken by Solomon were probably controlled by the murderers. It's interesting that if I arrive today there, it is Lali's or Saba's duty to walk the dog. Are they controlled too?

But it cannot work in this way... It's better if we arrange to watch out them by different people, they need to get dressed in exercise clothes and to have a ball with them. If they see me there again, they will have a doubt. I think, I am safe for now, they did not recognize me, because I had changed the image to the end. So was thinking Londa and she always did the same, what she thought about.

Besides of it, Londa was finally convinced that the

anonymous call author was not Solomon Kalandadze. Accordingly, the answer to the expertise is really interesting. She was thinking about new plans. Was difficult to choose which group to contact and how to explain it to them.

"But we'll have two rabbits, if the operative service starts to control from our side. – it is a delicate work and it needs a lot of thoughts to be involved in it people from outside, unknown from everyone in this system. Because in the murder case, whom with was fighting Mirza Qurdiani, could be involved some policemen, the same time, we know, that some policemen were in friendship with "Thieves in Law" and they unified the fight against Mirza Kurdiani. That's why the watching person should be a different person – not a thief or a policeman."

NEW PLANS

Londa made notes about two meetings for the next day. First, with her own group and the second meeting – with the operative workers.

She added to her group three new members: Eldar Topchiev, David Jinjolava and Mikheil Mamniashvili. They were great investigators. Among their friends was a joke about them: If they would find just only a bloody handkerchief, it was enough for them to investigate any kind of murder. Maybe they really had different experiences, which criminal matters needed.

Londa's plans approved. The group unanimously decided to meet with the operative staff to decide together about protecting the family members of the main witness, Solomon Kalandadze, for the purpose of their security, to determine who were spying on this family.

On the next day, they started watching over Solomon Kalandadze, his wife Lali Berikishvili and his son Saba Kalandadze. The time-table was taken from what Londa had studied: in the mornings between 8.009.00, and in the evenings at 20.00 till 21.00. Besides, they should control every movement of Solomon Kalandadze and his work schedule. It was not clear whether his working place knew or not about his witnessing of the murder of Mirza Kurdiani. One member of the operative group would be employed at Solomon's work, on the staff whose job would be to conduct daily examination of the work of the factory staff.

In addition, at the meeting, they decided to place front of Solomon Kalandadze's residential building a beer machine, where a person from their department would sell a beer and to watch what kind of people would be moving in that area. Also was planned to set up two benches opposite of Mirza Qurdiani's residential block.

Prior to that, Londa's group also planned watching from time to time for anything doubtful in the yard. One of them would take photos and the other would follow the suspicious person. They were assigned an old black car, on which was inscribed on the car's door: "Technical Assistance of vehicles" and also the phone numbers.

GUN SHOT AND THE BLACK BULLDOG

Ucha and Mirian, visited the area of Solomon Kalandadze's residence at 8 o'clock in the morning, as they were directed by the special forces. In the yard there was nobody near the house, just the sound of music on radio was heard from one of the first floor flat.

Ucha broke the silence and said to Mirian with humour:

I wonder, what is happening? Why is the whole yard so silent? It seems that the radio left on by some old Azeri man, as young people nowadays do not listen to such songs.

As if someone inside flat heard their talking, the curtains we removed and the windows were shut. Boys now missed even that hardly enjoyable "Baiati".

Suddenly, the black bulldog with white chest in a heart shape came out of the entrance and ran. A man followed it. Ucha and Mirian were confused, as they were expecting Mrs Lali today ... and asked each other: "should it not be a lady in the mornings?"

Mirian and Ucha were sitting in a car, and carefully were observing the dog and its owner. The man had exactly the same appearance as was described by Londa, and the Kalandadze's bulldog was black with a white heart.

There was no one in the street, except the yard keeper. The bulldog twice approached to the yard keeper. It was easy to guess that the yard keeper knew the dog but not its owner. It was natural, not astonishing, because in the mornings usually Lali was walking the dog.

The yard keeper said to the dog owner: – perhaps on Saturdays you aren't working and this is the reason you are here today with this dog?

Ucha got out from the car. He took a plastic container out from the car boot and went to the fountain to fill it. The fountain was hardly producing any water so it was impossible to fill his container.

Ucha asked the yard keeper:

Sir, do you know where to turn on the tap to increase the flow of water for the fountain?

The yard keeper drops his brush to the ground and went to Ucha. They found the tap but it was so rusted, they could not open it.

Solomon joined the conversation: It needs a special spanner, I must have it in my cellar, if you wait, I will get it right now.

He asked the yard keeper to look after "Chichi" and went to his basement.

Mirian also got out of the car, he opened the bonnet of the car and started looking inside it. Soon Solomon brought the tool and asked Ucha for his help. Mirian used the moment and approached them, trying to help them too.

Mirian, compared to Ucha, was eloquent and more sociable:

“Well, what help do you need?” Mirian asked.

The head of the tap was quite rusty. They were trying to repair it, but in vain. The water flowed down and the flow of water up was no longer supplied.

Solomon decided that this issue he would solve as soon as possible.

“What can I call you?” he asked the boys.

“Mirian and Ucha,” answered Mirian.

“And what is your name?” Mirian asked back him.

I am Solomon Kalandadze. I have been living in this building for 23 years and I think we have changed it just once. It’s good that you need the water, otherwise this fountain would run so poorly. Well, there to me came one idea, he continued, Would it be better if we put here a spring? – And let’s named it in respect of my tragically dead neighbor.

On hearing this, the light of joy came to the eyes of Ucha and Mirian and almost unanimously asked, who was his neighbor. It seemed that, Solomon wanted to talk about this issue. He all of a sudden raised the question with the boys and said:

One of our honest prosecutors lived here... yes, a member of the gang made an ambush and killed him. At first, he fired at him twice, and then the third one was the bullet, that killed him.

“And did you see it? How do you know it happened like that?” Mirian asked.

This question put Solomon in great emotions... but he still added with pretended natural reaction: was not necessary to see it, I heard, when I was coming home from my night shift. – Kalandadze replied with deep pain, as if he went into deep memory.

"Do you think the investigation goes on? I hope the investigation will find the killer," said Kalandadze.

As I know, Mirza Kurdiani was a highly qualified lawyer, a professor of Ivane Javakhishvili Tbilisi State University. He was killed by not a personal enemy, but the Georgian nation's enemy, – said Mirian.

How can I force myself to believe that no one from this two blocks saw who and how he was killed. I am surprised by the mentality of the Georgian man. Perhaps there is a witness, but they cannot trust anyone... and it is possible too, that they have a family, and it is too hard to admit the truth at this vulnerable time. – Ucha said joining in the conversation.

I would personally leave my work and protect the rights of such a witness. As you read in the Bible, "there is no secret that will not be revealed." This secret sooner or later will be revealed. The killers often admit the truth. – convincingly said Mirian. If citizens are defended, then the state and law are strong.

As far as I know, Mirza Qurdiani's deputy, Nikoloz Gabadadze did not occupy his job. He was being asked for it, but he did not move over the Christian morals until 40 days from the death of Mr. Mirza. Then he gathered the most powerful investigative personnel and honestly started the investigation. As I heard, the identity of the witness has been established, but they are not giving it away. They are cautious about him and he is protected. His family members are also watched over not to be hurt by bad people. – said Ucha and he had not completed his sentence, because attracted his attention two strangely dressed people, who had entered the entrance to the yard. Mirian took a look at how they were talking at the corner of the apartment building with the yard keeper. It did not look like a question and answer mode of conversation. It seemed that They were demanding from him some answers. Then he saw how he was talking to them with gestures. After that he stayed near them and continued cleaning the area. Then he suddenly disappeared. Mirian was afraid of the fact that Solomon Kalandadze could be in danger and they continued talking with him about building the spring. The same time they were playing with his bulldog. Solomon offered materials to the boys, because he liked the idea and called them to go to his basement to choose metal materials. The situation became tense. Somehow they wanted to take Solomon home safely. They realized that the witness was actively persecuted. Immediately, a multicolor car was parked near the building and three men were sitting in it. The yard keeper was walking to and fro. The situation became tense.

Mirian asked Solomon: Do you know him? I see him for the first time, – Kalandadze said. One person got out of the car and entered the second entrance. The other two were watching him from sideways of the yard.

The situation became much tenser. Solomon could not guess anything and he insistently was inviting the boys to his basement. The bulldog suddenly started barking and rushed into the entrance, where the sound of a gunshot was heard.

WOUNDED BULLDOG

The neighbors woke up at the sound of the gun shot. "Chichi" was lying in his own blood in the entrance and was crying and yelping. It was heartbreaking.

Mirian transmitted information to the duty group about the crime. The culprits did not come out of the entrance, they ran up to other floors. On the eighth floor a woman was taken hostage and she was taken to the roof of the building.

The police were on the scene. Special police officers arrived too. They were trying to get to the roof of the house.

One of the kidnappers called down to the police. They were not going to surrender and threatened to kill the lady.

On the photo, that was taken by Mirian, Londa identified both men. They were the men from the previous day, spying on Solomon and his family members.

Almost eight hours passed and the situation did not change.

Londa called an emergency meeting and ordered the operative workers to watch and to video everyone in the area. The hidden video was showing all new arrivals. Ucha suddenly noticed face of the yard keeper, who was not wearing special clothes and stood at the entrance. He moved to the entrance and was observing from nearby. Suddenly, some teenager approached to the yard keeper, and put into his pocket some paper. It seemed that he waited for some answer from him. The yard keeper was observing all people around, after he removed the letter from his pocket and read it. shortly after this he tried to break through the crowd and go to the street. Mirian and Ucha with the help of police officers arrested the yard keeper and the boy. Gathering people around started harassing saying why was arrested the poor yard keeper, but no one recognizes the boy.

THE SECRET LETTER

Londa urgently requested the questioning of the detainees. The yard keeper was kept isolated and was silent. In the letter which was found in his pocket, was threatening and commanding words written: “Before you don’t receive some sign from us, don’t move from there, in one hour start to act, otherwise we will not leave you alive”. The substance which was banned was removed from his pocket.

The boy who passed the letter to yard keeper was a teenager. He was terrified and convinced the police that he knew nothing. He was assuring the police, that in the street, an unknown man asked him to pass to the yard keeper a letter. When he was asked, where did he know the man from, he said that he first saw him.

The investigation left the two men in custody. It was difficult to identify the boy. He did not tell the truth about his surname and name or other data. In a few hours, all the data of the boy were identified and his parents were called for questioning.

Many people were on the scene. it got darker. The police asked to the criminals about releasing of the hostage through the megaphone, but in answer they were demanding their safe release.

Londa decided that they would not win with emotion and anger. One more sacrifice they could not accept. The mother of four young children had been taken as the hostage and they did not intend to let her free. Seemed, that criminals were quite mobilized. the woman who had been taken as the hostage had been reexamined, because her character was known by criminals. She was constantly calling her children and cried with panic with heart and begged the law enforcers to let criminals go free.

All limits of time have been exhausted. The woman had come to desperation. All channels of Georgian television were showing the situation live. The operative group was not allowed to use the helicopter because the criminals could kill the hostage. At least one clue was found in the investigation: the yard keeper and the little boy ...The police cleared all people from nearby the residential building and from the eighth floor to the first was arranged security corridor. The criminals did not consider reliability of this offering and demanded to make free the whole block of building. It was done so, but the decision could not finally be agreed. After consulting the operative group decided to act differently. They decided to take the inner glass on the ceiling and to use the tear gas. But for this needed to find a person living there, who would know of the attic vents. The operative service found that the military training engineer lived on the eighth floor of the second entrance, a lonely man, who was in the service at the same time. Immediately was sent to him an Operator Service Inspector to plan in there how to act.

From the roof the woman's panic screaming no longer heard, something was done sneakily. The police were calling by the megaphone to the woman, but no voice was coming from roof any more. The situation became very tense. There was a single shot on the roof, but the lady's voice still was not heard. In the meantime, the neighboring army officer was brought. With his help was made an agreement with other neighbors and police officers and they all entered the flat, where could be placed the went to the roof. There were mobilized three emergency medical aid vehicles, fire brigade crew and emergency services at the site.

Soon operation on the roof started. Not to have doubt criminals, by megaphone they were offered various offers, but the criminals the sign of negative answer were giving fire in the air. After a little time, there was again the hostage woman's screaming. Maria relieved deeply, the hostage was alive. On the roof soon was spread the smell of the gunpowder. It was already dark night. With the support of the Ministry of Energy and Natural Resources the operation service has turned off energy in the entire settlement. Maria asked for patience from the people. Little and would be an end of this terrible scenario.

Within 1015 minutes, the request of electric power was required by megaphone from the roof.

The operation ended perfectly. The patients were moved with care to the emergency service car. Among them were all participants in the operation with signs of poisoning.

Two days later, Londa's group returned the hostage mother to her children.

DO NOT SEEK AN ANGEL IN MAN

At 10 am Londa invited the investigative group. All TV channels of Georgia were gathered in the reception of the General Prosecutor's Office. Naturally, there are questions from society when they see strange behavior from the criminals. Mass Media was interested in first of all criminals, the health of the woman taken hostage and the fate of the wounded bulldog.

Naturally, four prisoners were found in the preliminary detention setting. Investigation has undoubtedly made some specific progress. Although the identity of the main witness was established, the main issue was the identity of the killers. They were spread like metastasis among innocent people and no one knew how much damage they would cause them.

Operative service was carefully monitored Mirza Kurdiani's residential building and its surroundings. According to the plan, a beer seller was installed and a new yard keeper was assigned.

Londa could not sleep all night. Insomnia attacked her. She constantly was thinking about the fate of Solomon Kalandadze and his family members. All the workers involved in these operative actions should be very cautious. She remembered an expression saying: "the fortress breaks from inside". It was a possible danger. all members of the Prosecution team were reliable, but anyway needed to be careful. Prosecution team was absolutely loyal, but she had doubt of members of other groups. was there anyone unreliable, a betrayer? Then they could be all vulnerable. Gradually she was convinced in the wisdom of Kalandadze's family, that they were not expressing about killer's identity.

Indeed, their lives were in danger. This terrible pain was common to law enforcers, civilians, and these three healthy people, the members of one family.

The criminals were spying with great caution on the witness's family.

Londa Finally was convinced that they were trying to destroy Kalandadze's family members every day in a permanent manner. She was thinking about radical events, but it was still early. It was not excluded that the guilty party would have been temporarily exhausted, but then they needed to work ten times harder. It was a topic that could not be resolved in a narrow circle. It was necessary to have a secret meeting with the secret consultation on the security of Kalandadze's family and another thousand issues that are high on the Prosecutor General's Office in the elite circle resolved.

With the questioning of Solomon Kalandadze, she would not get anything new. Londa knew for sure that the witness did not know the identity of the murderer, he could only recognize him! On the identification of the main person they were working day after day.

To Londa appeared hidden fear. Needed to be saved not just the witness's family, but her and her family too. She remembered that she should not search an angel in the person, but she would easily find Satan. Those people who were involved in this scenario would have all been doomed as soon as they would made a little mistake.

From prosecutors' media center The journalists only found out that the guilty had been accused of wounding the bulldog and later developments. in The public motioned conception that some two men were helping the kidnappers in the kidnapping of the bulldog. Since the bulldog bit one of them, it was wounded. The reason for arresting of the yard keeper was just it, that he was helping thieves.

NEW WAYS

Londa went to meet the yard keeper the next morning. On her way there she felt tense. She had to meet the man, who, possibly, knew everything about the murder. He seemed a little naive. Did criminals really rely on this yard keeper? Did they trust him with such an important secret? Did they forced him to do such things by intimidation? – Londa was disturbed by such thoughts. Maybe this young man is involved in this case just then when they need him. Interestingly, what is the connection of that little boy with this matter? how they know each other? – Many questions were bothered Londa. He will have to answer for the serious crime, as there was a threat of intimidation involving of an adolescent to this matter. An explosive substance that was taken out of his pocket, was taken in his hands from a juvenile, or received from his hand. Londa remembered that the boy gave him a letter. It's also interesting. Was this only a letter or it was an explosive substance? Then the charge of the yard keeper could be more aggravated, as he knew that the juvenile was pushed for a serious crime.

Londa's thoughts were disturbed just then when the auto inspector stopped and fined her for violating traffic rules. But when the Inspector recognized her, he brought his hand to his forehead and let her go with honor.

Londa Amilakhvari ordered an appointment for the detained Sergi Menabde in the preliminary detention center... as, usually, it happened. In the meantime, as she had to wait for the prisoner half an hour, Londa consulted with Bagatur Kukuladze, the head of the Operative Service. Speaking about Sergi Menabde, Bagatur said that Sergy had a solid understanding of the three languages: Russian, Azeri and Armenian and he spoke with his coprisoners in their own languages without any accent. Sergy did not tell to prisoners that he was the yard keeper. His detention he considered as a mistake. Londa was happy and satisfied with this news, saluted Bagator and asked him not to take his eyes from Sergy.

Sergy was already waiting for Londa in the questioning room. He looked overwhelmed. He was not pleased to see her. It seemed that he already knew Londa's principle character.

Interrogation began:

"Tell me your biography briefly, if you can," Londa asked him and prepared a pen and paper.

Sergy began:

I was born in Tbilisi, in 1960. I have grown up in Mtatsminda district, and on Arsena's road I got plenty of close friends. I spent all my youth together with them. We were as parts of each other's families. The doors of our houses had never been closed. We walked in the doors without knocking. We had shared each other's sorrows and joys.

I graduated from high school 51 and the same year I

became as a student of the university. Then I worked at a military academy as a teacher. – continued Sergy.

"Why do you work as a yard keeper and how long it has been happening?" asked Londa.

It seemed that the offender expected this question and immediately gave an explanation:

I worked at the military academy for six months as I already told you. After I became unemployed on account of cutting down on staff and I did not refuse the first opportunity to save my family.

"Who helped you find this job?" Londa asked suddenly.

Gizo Khomeriki, an employee of the military academy, helped me to find this job.

Are you officially employed as a cleaner of the state?

I was not able to come to the state, but when they need me, they call me.

Is the salary paid by the call?

No, salaries sometimes Gizo Khomeriki gives me.

How much do they pay at each call?

It depends on the kind of work. Sometimes we clean big areas, I cannot say about my payment, it is secret of organization. I'd like to keep this as firm's secret.

As you see, you are not alone in this job. is there yet another?

At this question, Sergy confused:

Sometimes I'm with another.

Who else is it, if is not the secret of the firm? – Londa did not stop.

I do not think he's in the state, either.

Tell me, how are you going, where are you going, who is

calling you, is that person your acquaintance, familiar, with whom you are working?

The yard keeper became very confused by such questions and angrily screamed at Londa:

What's connection has with my cleaning business when I leave home, whom will I meet and who pays me?

Why are you worrying? you need to justify the truth. you want to prove your innocence, don't you? so it's better to answer all my questions. Just with this way you can get out free from here.

I will answer you... – with the man, that Gizo brought to me, I worked just three times. His name is Zaza. I do not remember his surname well; I think it is Khuluzauri. One person comes to us and brings cleaning staff, inventory and special clothes.

Is Zaza an old employee, or he is like you without state, not on the staff?

I think he is not on the staff. He is a lawyer, how I remember, he is well educated in law.

"Do you talk about laws the time of working?" Londa astonishingly asked.

Yes, when we finish our job we have a lot of time before inventory car arrives.

Is it the same vehicle or different? and do you remember the driver's name and surname? or phone number?

Yes, why not. At the previous meeting he took us to a restaurant, he is known as Suliko Jankhoteli and his brother is working in the police department.

Does the brother of the chief of police department work as a cleaner?

No, he doesn't clean, but he serves us with his own car.

"Who's paying for him the salary?" Londa asked cynically.

Salaries, I've already told you, Gizo Khomeriki pays, – he said these words and seemed that he wanted to speak more, but something was stopping him. Londa guessed, that the interrogation rules and the so-called methods should be immediately changed.

After a short pause she offered to Sergy Menabde cigarette, which she removed from her bag, it was cigarette "Cosmos". Londa lit him it and started to smoke herself too. She was not a smoker. For a while, these two were silent. After their silence interrupted Londa's unendurable cough. Sergi noticed that she was not a smoker and immediately asked:

Have you been smoking for a long time?

No, my mother has just died and I smoke cigarettes on nervous ground.

I do not recommend if you have especially children at home, – Sergy was working on the sign of devotion.

Londa remembered the words one of her colleagues: if you wish to hear the truth from the witness, advise cigarette and the same time accompany him, smock with him, and you got it. With cigarette you can have coffee and like that will create certain relationship between you and the witness. Remembering this, Londa asked the supervisor to bring them two coffees. the conversation between Sergy and Londa developed in more warm atmosphere.

Some time ago you mentioned about the policeman Jankhoteli, have you ever seen this person? – asked by the way Londa.

If I knew that you do not tell my secret, I would say, but I prefer to stay in jail than in the ground.

Londa was silent for a while, and she preferred silence. Sergy continued to talk about the same issue.

As if he wanted more loyalty from Londa, but her face started to express more offence.

Londa, I will say more, because I trust you. Sometimes police officer Gaga Jankhoteli meets me and he pays me small wages too. He is also supporting me, and I do not know why, but he is often asking about the owner of the black bulldog, Kalandadze's family. He asks me to pass him information about their movement and their guests too. I remembered, that you came twice with the Spaniel dog and talked once with a neighbor woman and I could not guess that time who you were. The second time you spoke with black bulldog owner Kalandadze itself quite a long time. I pretended to clean the yard. If you want true, you were talking too quietly and I could not hear you, just Kalandadze once pointed to the Mirza Qurdiani's house and show his sorrow. That's all... and all about these knows Jankhoteli too. "Which of the Jankhoteli brothers knows about this?" asked Londa.

"Of course, it's Gaga Jankhoteli, a police officer," Sergy replied with dividing into syllables.

"Now we have learned so much of each other's secret, you won't hide nothing from me. Perhaps he expressed an interest about me," said by the troubled Londa. The same time she noticed that he wanted to say more and more, everything what he knew about. Londa consciously looked at the clock and got anxious. Sergy fell for the bait and asked to Londa:

Londa, please, continue the meeting time and stay with me. I am in mood to say what's true. I know you are interesting in it too. The same time I want to ask you to be more cautious, as they are watching at you personally. Gaga Jankhoteli knows all your steps.

Yes, but why such a noble man like you in exchange for money, working for such a bad man?

I am a victim, Londa, what can I do? If they have a small doubt about my betrayal, they will immediately get rid of me.

Why do you talk in plural, Gaga is one... and who are you scared of more.

No, not only Gaga there. A few people are gathering in a two room apartment on Gagarin square and have secret meetings there.

"Do they coming there dressed as policemen?" asked Londa.

No, they are not policemen but I think they are the thieves of law.

How does a policeman meet legitimate thieves alone?

No, sometimes others are coming too. but I do not know the names but I know their faces. Sometimes they are staying there until morning and drinking cognac.

"Have you heard about me in this circle," asked Londa.

Yes, they are watching on you for a long time, be cautious about everything.

Londa was shocked, but did not show him.

One of the thief is called "scissors", so I'm afraid of him too. Let's help each other.

Londa friendly warned Sergy not to have contact and

trust with any one and to have only superficial relationships with his cocellers.

Londa received a lot of information from Sergy, but the confidence rate was low, so she warned the operative department to oversee him.

Londa came out excited from the investigative isolation. The fate of Sergi Menabde worried her greatly. She felt that the distance was getting closer to the murderers. She approached with her car keys in her hand to her car and became very embarrassed and surprised when she saw her "Mercedes" – instead of tires was standing on the bricks.

Thus, this way was warned Londa Amilakhvari by criminals.

LONDA'S BIRTHDAY

It was the daybreak of February 23rd, and it was Londa's birthday. Her mother was just passed away and she did not think to celebrate her birth day. She constantly felt sorrowful.

Londa loved French realist writer Emil Zola. She constantly remembered his words: "If you hide the truth and bury it into the ground, it will certainly grow up and it will destroy everything in its path."

But people do not change, changes only demanding of time. The truth is only one and false are thousands, but if you fight for the truth, you will find that one way and you will like it very much, that you will never try to get out of this way, as the right path is godly and true. Perhaps if a man who lies just once admits the truth after lying, even he will like it so much, he probably will never turn to the wrong path again.

Lie... is it necessary to deceive others?... no, people often deceive just themselves. Some people take stupefying drugs, because they do not want to realize reality. Some people lose on gambling games, and here is double standard lying – lies to himself and to others too... and of course, even a double standard lie deceives himself and deceives others... and there are lots of other things that are found every day. The society is divided into three parts: Some are lying, the second part stays deceived, and the third part – who judges them for their actions.

Londa Amilakhvari fell into philosophical issues. She did not want to turn back, and did not want either to think deeply about the people, who made such nastiness for Sergy Menabde's thugs.

The incident of car tires the matter that left her car without tires, was quite disturbing. Because she felt insecure. Londa had a strong psyche and thus acted in a foreseen situation.

She thought that Sergy Menabde would be more vulnerable outside. He needed help. At this stage, the prison regime would be more protected than outside from robbers, until all of them would be sentenced.

The phone ringing made Londa jump... Her father was congratulating on her birthday. Other calls followed quickly and finally her friends invited her with her family to the restaurant "Kolkheti". Londa did not resist. She was pleased with friends' decision.

Londa found an unforgettable surprise. She was given by her friends her own poetry book. Londa was constantly hiding her poems, as Georgia is the country of poetry, she thought, her poems would be weak compared to others.

There at the table were gathered her poetry appraisers. The journalists of press and television were invited too at her birthday table. The editor of the newspaper "Resonance" awarded Londa with title of poet prosecutor's status.

From this day Londa became as a poet prosecutor. Appeared that many colleagues were writing too, including the country's general prosecutor – Nugzar Gabrichidze, after whose death was published his poems by his colleagues.

Londa's colleagues Tamaz Iaseishvili, Temur Moniava, Ia Kipiani, Otar Burduli, Koki Narmania and others were poem writers too. Also Judges Vaja Qacanashvili, Mtvarisa Tchevlishvili, Lotbert kupatadze and the first Deputy of Supreme Court Guguli Devdariani.

So that, Georgia is indeed a country of miracles. Almost all Georgians live with poetry and in the most difficult situations, they are helped by poetry. So, there is a constant battle needed to grow spiritually. Whoever don't like to fight, go against themselves and fall in to the abyss.

BLOOD PUDDLE IN THE 54TH CELL

At dawn, the alarm went off in the prison. Worried prisoners called upon officers to take care of them. The blood was in the cell and the prisoners were looking at Sergy Menabde, who was lying on the floor with vein cut hands without any sign of life. There were 6 prisoners in the cell. According to international standards, cell should have been 24 square meters, but this was roughly abrogated of the norm. In the cell, it felt very stuffy.

Immediately, the door was opened and in the threshold

4 officers appeared. Prisoners quickly took their places. It happened very quickly. Sergy was lying on the floor and there was no sign of life. Officers came with prison hospital surgeon, who demanded space. The doctor checked the pulse and examined the eyes. Sergy had lost a large amount of blood, he was unconscious. The doctor demanded to move him immediately to hospital. She did not wait to fill any protocol, as there was no more time. The patient was on the verge of life and death. By the initiation of doctor Manana Sergy was moved to the city's strongest surgical center.

The doctor on duty appeared, he turned out, to be a young sympathetic surgeon Zaza Kobulia. The patient was immediately rushed to the operating table.

Sergy was the most serious patient in the hospital. Londa demanded to strengthen his defenses. The life of Sergy should be preserved for two reasons: First, the life of a young man was in danger and, secondly, he had important information. Through him would be unmasked a lot of dirt.

"MAN IS A WOLF FOR A MAN!"

It is a formula of selfishness and a greedy person, and this greedy person is, indeed, extremely dangerous to society.

Londa was shocked by what had happened. The investigation, that was linked to the incident, began. But who, who had led Sergy to that extent? Did he attempt suicide? "Did I give a reason for that?" Londa thought: "Did anyone use his coceller as a companion? Or had he met someone after me who might have pushed him, or was it an insidious plan to get him out of the hospital?" Londa Amilakhvari thought so, when her cell phone rang and she was informed that Sergy was trying to make contact with his life.

The Investigation Department of the Ministry of Justice has launched an investigation into the attempted "suicide" in prison. The investigation was supervised by the Office of the Prosecutor General.

Unfortunately, the period coincided with the lack of expert technical means in the area of investigation. There was no video eye and no cells were recorded. Only through the testimony of witnesses and the murder weapon, the knife itself, was it possible to establish the truth.

No, Londa could not give up her position ... no one should know what was going on between him and Sergy Menabde, what they were talking about. Therefore, she demanded to be involved in the investigative team. At the same time, she should have questioned people, who named Sergy. Suliko Jankhoteli would go first to be questioned. In the second row, the boy who handed to Sergy a letter and the explosive powder, was interrogated. Should be interrogated also criminals from the roof of the Solomon's house. The investigation has entered an interesting phase. The circle of criminals was increasing day by day and new victims were expected every day. Therefore, the investigative team had to act swiftly, but cautiously.

CHIEF DOCTOR

Londa wanted to talk to the chief doctor. They arranged the time and now she was restlessly looking forward to meeting him. She found out that Vepkhia Tsiklauri was an apolitical person and at the same time he was known as a first class doctor. He condemned the misconduct, which was unfortunately common in hospital staff.

Londa knocked on the door carefully. Mr. Vepkhia had just finished doing his rounds and made his way to his office. He invited Londa in to his office with courtesy.

Londa broke the silence and asked him:

Have you got a lot patient?

Yes, – replied the doctor.

Is Zaza Kobulia, Resuscitation Doctor, experienced?

He has been two years in surgery and now we have moved him there, in resuscitation section.

Will he be competent to save Sergy Menabde? He's the patient in the worse condition.

Yes, of course.

I have one request; can you personally take under your care Sergy Menabde? The cause of his injury is still unclear, and it is therefore dangerous to leave him alone for a minute.

Well, you know, I guess all, I heard and we will definitely

take action. But the guard is guarding him and they are responsible for his safety. As for healing, we do our very best.

And yet... I have one request that no one from the staff should be allowed to going into his room without your permission. Please permanently put a trusted nurse over of him.

I have learned everything. We will adhere to all norms of safety.

Londa was happy to say goodbye to Tsiklauri and landed on the stairs to Sergy's room. During the resuscitation, the guard watched over the entire floor. Londa accidently collided with a nurse at the door, who was taking a quick step towards the patient.

"One minute!" she stopped her.

"Yes, I am listening!" answered a nurse and nervously corrected her hat.

Did you get permission to be in here? – No, because it is my duty.

Please note that the patient is accused and do not go in without the permission of the chief physician.

"Who are you?" the nurse asked.

Londa Amilakhvari, investigator of this case.

Upon hearing this, the nurse seemed eager to say something, but refrained. Londa noticed the nurse was hiding something, but the conversation continued as usual.

What is your name? Londa asked.

Lia, Lia Navrozashvili.

Lia, my dear, please cooperate, as it is about the health of the young man. We can see that even the walls of the prison did not secure him and he appeared in such a difficult situation. Please be careful as well ... someone, I mean his enemy, might want to get closer to you, let me know about it. However, it is better to listen to everything and give them an answer after telling me.

How's that? – What can I tell them at that moment? – Tell them that you will think.

Understandable, can I enter in now?

Let's get together now. – Londa said.

The patient was very disturbed. It seemed his body was trying hard to return to life. Londa was given hope. She was still observing the patient for a while, wanting to witness the moment when Sergy would opened his eyes. Then she asked the nurse once again to tell her all the news immediately. Eventually, they exchanged business cards as a sign of friendship and cooperation and said goodbye to each other.

INTERROGATION OF SULIKO JANKHOTELI

The criminals, arrested on the roof of Mirza Kurdiani's residence did not testify. They chose the right to remain silent. Londa had to question Suliko Jankhoteli.

Jankhoteli was summoned to the General Prosecutor's Office at 10 am.

This guy was a pretty interesting man ... even dressed in the latest fashion, and he drove an expensive car. Londa has collected a lot of information about him. Suliko had serious links with suspected men and was involved in the gambling business, as he had his own shares in it. People of all kinds of understanding regularly gathered there and half of Georgia's fate was planned there. It was also possible, that Mirza Kurdiani's murder was planned there.

In addition, Londa had a lot more information. She decided to meet Suliko Jankhoteli with her group member Dudu Arziani. Londa gave some information to Dudu and warned him that if any question arose, such a question would only occur after agreeing with her. Suliko was a geologist by profession, and he was remarkably cautious.

Londa and Dudu were talking when Goga ZavraDashvili knocked on her door and looked carefully into her office.

I'll tell you one word and I'll leave you, Goga said.

Come in! – Dudu and Londa invited him at the same time.

Recently, Gaga Jankhoteli spoke to our colleagues and asked him to find out what was causing his brother to be summoned to the prosecutor's office. He also demanded that Suliko be questioned after several days. Otherwise, he would appeal to the Attorney General.

Let us turn to the Attorney General and then question Jankhoteli. – said angrily Londa.

We have to question him for every reason today – Dudu Arziani said.

Prosecutor's Office did not heed or accept Gaga Jankhoteli's request.

The interrogation began.

Suliko Jankhoteli was being questioned as a witness. The answer to the first question positively or negatively would be both equally interesting.

After answering the necessary questions, Londa asked:

Do you know Sergy Menabde?

Yeah, I've known him for about three years.

How did you meet and under what circumstances?

He was introduced by our mutual friend Gizo Khomeriki.

Who is Gizo Khomeriki and how do you know him?

Gizo Khomeriki My brother, Gaga, introduced me to him... where and how I can no longer remember.

What did you have in common with Gizo and Sergy?

Nothing important. I'm a casino's owner and Sergy loves gambling, that's all.

Your brother loves gambling too?

He loves, but he defends his dignity of his uniform and does not play.

However, though he is often your guest?

He is my brother and of course. We can no longer meet him in the family and occasionally comes here, but let me tell you he is not playing.

Do you know anyone called "Scissors"?

Of course, I know him from my brother.

How... did your brother introduce you to him? – Asked the surprised Dudu.

Yeah, he caught him a couple of years ago, now they are friends, he's a cool client.

Is "Scissors" a Law Thief? – Yes, even kids know it.

Do you know why "scissors" was caught then, or by whom?

Of course, by the order of the prosecutor, Mirza Kurdiani.

Did you know Mirza Kurdiani? – Yes, I knew him.

Did you know him by sight?

I met him several times for various events.

Did Sergy Menabde know about him too?

No, I don't know, I really know that he didn't know him from me.

Where did Sergy work, don't you know? – At the Military Academy.

Didn't he get another jobs?

Suliko Jankhoteli hesitated to answer this question, as

if he could not remember something. After he said quietly, his eyes fluttered and whispered:

This is a little embarrassing, but it was difficult for Sergy Menabde to work at the academy, he had money problem and he was also working in the second shift, as a yard keeper. I felt sorry for him and visited him with my car. I even gave my own money him out of my pocket several times.

And... Gizo Khomeriki didn't feel sorry for him?

Yes, Gizo did also the same, of course, he is a generous man.

From his own pocket?

I don't really know... how to tell you that I was actually financing Gizo and my brother.

Do you know the shoe factory engineer?

No, where from?

Do you know whom about I am asking?

I don't know ... – Suliko was confused.

Do you know Solomon Kalandadze?

No, I don't know.

Jankhoteli was lying this time. Londa strongly reminded him that false testimony was punishable.

What should I know and why?

Did not Sergy Menabde tell you about Solomon Kalandadze?

You mean Soliko, the owner of the Bulldog?

Yes, Soliko!

Did you bring special clothes to the yard keeper?

When?

How many times have you delivered?

I don't remember how many times, but I used to get some tools and clothes and then took them home.

Did you come to the scene of the incident when Menabde was performing his duties?

Before the incident, I went and took him the clothes broom and scoop.

All this is constantly stored in your car?

Yes.

As it became known to the investigation, you send special clothes with Aziza Muradov?

No, I did not send any special clothes.

What did you send with the boy? – asked Londa. – I don't remember. I think only clothes.

Maria and Dudu strongly warned him once again about giving false testimony, after which the interrogation continued:

As Aziz Muradov says you gave him a letter and something to hand over to the yard keeper, and you left the area immediately.

Well, boy, he is mentally ill and it seems hallucinations started, I did not send anything else with him, – Suliko growled.

How do you know that he is sick? – seems from his appearance.

Exactly?

He is lying, I told you he has hallucinations.

And, Menabde? has got hallucinations too? – Dudu Arziani asked him with raised voice.

What? and did Menabde say that I have sent with Azizah's hand any other item for him?

Jankhoteli could no longer explain what he had sent with Aziza's hand and he realized that he was trapped.

I can contradict you Menabde, he will tell the truth,

good that the law gives me the right to confront and I will use it.

No, Menabde wouldn't say that, I can't believe it, – Suliko Jankhoteli spoke in a confused and troubled voice.

Moreover, before your interrogation began, your brother informed us that you knew the truth, and we had to question you critically.

What is happening? Is my brother cheating on me too?

No one betrayed you, if you tell the truth, you will be released. If the substance you sent to Sergy Menabde, was given to you by your brother, it turns out that they needed it for the investigation. Have you sent some substance to Sergy by the boy's hand? Did you know that the substance was not actually explosive or poisonous, your brother tested Sergy Menabde, and he only wondered if Sergy Menabde would use it, and he checked to see if he was trusted? It was simply a test of loyalty.

It's not just Sergy, it turns out that my real brother, took the test on me too, I was convinced that the substance I gave Sergy was not explosive, but a poison.

Did Sergy know what you sent? Londa asked.

Of course he knew, but unfortunately he couldn't use it ... as I heard from you, it wasn't dangerous.

If you know that this scene was staged by your brother because the investigation needed it so.

No, of course, not... why should I have known, it turns out, my brother was using me as a blindfolded weapon.

No, your brother was well aware that Solomon Kalandadze witnessed the assassination of Mirza Kurdiani, and that's why it took so many secret observations.

–Yes, Solomon Kalandadze had witnessed the murder of

Qurdiani, but my people warned him not to say anything about it.

Who warned him? – I knew that too. Sergy recognized me when I went in for questioning with him. He told me that he saw me in the yard, when I was talking with Solomon Kalandadze, – continued Londa.

Suliko Jankhoteli was completely confused, he was surprised about how he was trapped by his own brother. He regretted not knowing the nature of his brother. Why he couldn't understand about his plan.

No, how do I know? ... Our duty was just to watch him, nothing more. My brother asked me and that's why I was doing it.

Do you know that Sergy is in the hospital, sir? Dudu asked suddenly.

Yes, I know he's in the hospital, but there he is guarded and I can't go to see him. They are said to be out of touch and he is in the most difficult situation.

Who says? Asked Londa.

Local medical staff.

Do you know anyone face to face there?

Yes, the nurse is my neighbor.

Lia Navrozashvili is your neighbour?

Yes, nobody, except her, can visit Sergy. If Sergy heals, he will probably confirm my statement.

Londa asked for time and went outside. She immediately contacted the chief doctor and asked him, to send nurse Lia Navrozashvili on a compulsory holiday.

The chief physician without any words understood the reason for Londa's request and agreed with the proposal.

Londa returned to the interrogation, Suliko Jankhoteli

was quietly answering questions. Her conversation revealed that he had a daily relationship with Lia Navrozashvili. She was closer to Gaga, that is, she reported daily to Gaga Jankhotel about the health of Sergy Menabde. Therefore, Gaga and her friends took care of Sergy, provided him with medical supplies, and instead promised Lia Navrozashvili a light sentence for her brother in prison.

Jankhoteli was not left in pretrial cell, as the investigation was interested in his every movement. They arranged to keep him under observation.

INTERROGATION OF A MINOR

A juvenile was questioned from the investigative team by Koka. Early in the morning the boy was interrogated, attended by Aziz Muradov's grandmother and lawyer Gia Tkeshelashvili. The situation was unusual, because Aziz was totally inexperienced and also mentally disabled. In the conversation, Koka noticed a low intelligence on the edge, which required a psychiatric examination. He was illiterate and often showed inadequacy. There was only one thing he could tell from the truth ... the fact that criminals were buying cigarettes and giving him pocket money... he did not know the names of those individuals ... but he remembered both of them. One of them seemed to be called Sergy, sometimes called Sergio, sometimes Seroja. Grandmother silently told the investigator that Aziza had twice tried to hang himself.

Koka requested isolation of the prisoner on the basis of this information and the next day he applied to the Levan Samkharauli Forensics Bureau for psychiatric examination on Aziz Muradov.

TROUBLE IN THE HOSPITAL

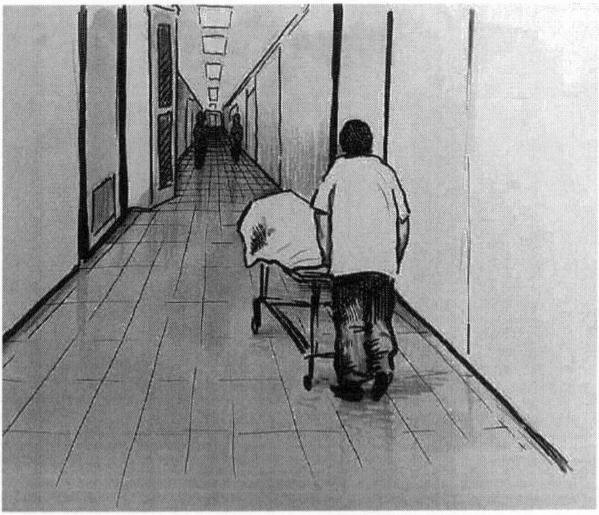

The wounded patient was taken to hospital at 6 am. The patient was accompanied by a large crowd. On the eighth floor of the hospital was Sergy Menabde's ward, the guard was inspecting. On the door of Sergy's room doctor's instruction was posted that no patients, even medical staff, would be allowed to enter the ward without administrative permission. Only the nurse, Ms. Lia Navrozashvili, was allowed to act independently beyond this statement. Lia was asked to change her twenty-four-hour shift and was given to her a resting room too.

The newly wounded man was undergoing surgery and, since there was no other way for the hospital administration, he was placed in the resuscitation ward. The room was located next to Sergy Menabde's chamber, where the administration's order was strictly enforced. Lia second patient was also added to the list. The concern has more than doubled. As Lia had promised to Londa, she rang her and let her know that in hospital was brought heavily wounded patient Suliko Jankhoteli, and he was placed next to Sergy's room as he had been hospitalized.

Londa was shocked hearing this horrible news, she was extremely strained. How could they not protect this man? The investigation failed to interrogate him for the second time, events were developing at such a lightning speed. Is it the same handwriting? Did Sergy and Janxoteli were wounded by same group? Is it a coincidence? or are the villains continuing the series of murder? She thought. Londa immediately called the meeting, and told the staff about the incident. Other people who were also in Sergy's circle friends were they also vulnerable? According to the plan, Suliko Jankhotel's brother, Gaga Jankhotel, was to be questioned ... and military academy officials, including Gizo Khomeriki, should also be questioned.

The Prosecutor General's Office has launched an investigation into Suliko Jankhoteli's "attempted murder under article."

GIZO KHOMERIKI DISAPPEARED

Londa with the group decided that at 10 am the next morning Gizo Khomeriki should be questioned. The witness was summoned, but it appeared that Khomeriki had disappeared. He had left no message at work, or it was possible also that his companions warned him to leave. Londa informed the Border Police about this person, but the border police told her that Gizo Khomeriki had already crossed the border into the Republic of Turkey. A search was announced for Gizo Khomeriki in Turkey.

AN IMPORTANT WITNESS

Investigation team resumed. They worked all night to avoid making an irreparable mistake again. Londa had a trump card preserved. From interrogation of Sergy Menabde she remembered someone of Khuluzauri, whom no one touched yet. However, she intended to interrogate Suliko Jankhoteli further. But Suliko was in a very bad condition. Londa now hoped just on the new witness. She hoped that the new witness would fill the gaps in Suliko's testimony.

In the interrogation of Khuluzauri, she would see the climax of the investigation, and climax will not be obtained without a fight, she knew it well. She had no right to make another mistake. A mistake would be a crime in this case. As soon as they transfer him an invitation from the Prosecutor's Office, Khuluzauri immediately disappears from the area, hiding. The investigation will be deadlocked. It is possible that those in the hospital who are in the resuscitation department may not even live. Everything needs to be calculated, and what concerns the juvenile Aziz Muradov, there will probably an assault or limited assault. At the time of committing the crime, no one doubted about his heath situation. So he won't even be a witness.

And lastly ... there is only Londa who owns this fateful

information. Who knows what they think of her, those bandits and sellers of their own homeland ... will they revenge her or her family members? Are there any dangers wait for her children who go to school without protection? Could his son get out of football training, or the girls in the children's dance classes. Can Londa control them permanently? She can get from government some protection from school to home, but they are adults and would this protection be enough? you cannot limit it. How much fun would her children miss because of her work? ... sometimes they can be hungry, sometimes they run into things in the yard, and where is their ever missing mother? There should be some state support for the people, like Londa. Londa is a state prosecutor and she is working for justice on behalf of the state. There should be some protection mechanisms that will make her family safer.

Londa restricted her children to excursions and leisure activities. They were growing up in harsh conditions. None of the parents in Londa's position, nor their children, who were willingly or unwillingly engaged in the endless work of their mother's prosecution service, did not receive any help from the new government. And worst of all, even Londa's salary was symbolic and it was impossible to hire a private teacher. It wasn't even possible to raise wages. There is such a tendency in Georgia, if you do not complain about the old government, you will never get a job. So whatever you do with your efforts, you should be able to protect yourself. But when you have to live in the bullseye of injustice and see that your compatriot is in need of you, like Alexander Chekhov's hero, sometimes he has tea and sometimes sugar. And you feel the advantage that you both have, you can never allow yourself to think better. At this time, you will be restrained even know restrained people may be more gifted than you are.

Another sleepless night ... fears, doubts, contradictions and ... who knows why Londa didn't have to overcome this one night. She could not trust anyone except her own intuition. Even intuitively, she felt that her enemies were even more numerous and wealthy.

Londa first went to the hospital where souls were fighting and no one knew when their heart beatings would stop. She watched their faces for hours, and they didn't have any signs of life. No optimism, Londa was overcome by a terrible misery ... Due to her profession, she had to constantly live between death and sadness. Londa never missed any chance of human support if she was given a chance. For Sergy, she did her maximum, to save him, she asked for help to immigrants living abroad to send her the brain nourishing drugs that was not available in Georgia that time, but unfortunately this effort was unsuccessful.

What a pity when you fight in the most vulnerable world of criminals as innocent and want to save your job, your family and your homeland, and in this clash, your own, coworker, who looks as if he fights alongside you but stabs you in the back. Is this a double gravity crime? While your teacher is being killed, prosecutor and investigative activities patriarch, Georgian prosecutor's conscience and honour, it becomes very difficult to even think about your own safety.

Londa was desperate to get out of the hospital, even thinking that Gizo Khomeriki, who should have been questioned as a witness, had gone away. It was possible that criminals got rid of him. It is difficult to control the situation of a cross border man, when a group of criminals everywhere have access, they are financed by mafia groups, and bribery shines on all kinds of "hell" on earth.

Londa had to go to the planned operation alone ...

At 2 am several shots were fired while she was driving away from Ninoshvili Street ...

Officers, experts and ambulances arrived at the scene rapidly...

End of the first part.

LONDA AMILAKHVARI AT THE HOSPITAL

Londa Amilakhvari, the investigator of important cases, was taken to hospital by ambulance. She was wounded in her shoulder by the criminals. Experts found three bullet holes at the accident scene. This time, the killer failed to kill the target, a reason could be lack of professionalism, or they had a different plan.

Londa didn't lose her mind even for a second. She was reluctant to speak due to severe stress, though she could speak. She was alone in the resuscitation ward, which gave her a quiet time to think. Her wish was not to avenge the attacker. Londa desperately wished to get better and continue her investigation. She was afraid, she may be dropped from this case, because of her injuries. So, she wanted to recover in time and get back to work.

Journalists gave a fairly broad and fair assessment of the attack on Londa, but the yellow press still circulated thousands of false rumors.

However, she has always remembered talking to wise crimes prosecutor Koki Narmania. On one occasion, an angry Londa asked Mr. Koki, why they were not taking action to report the lies and of lying reporters:

It possible, that any false publicity destroys your entire future? – Londa couldn't hide her anger.

Mr. Koki replied very wisely:

To admit blatant and defamatory misconduct by law enforcement agencies, including the Prosecutor's Office, of its inability and weakness to name its criminal offenses and to prevent a dangerous criminal event for the State and society. But most importantly, the political reporting of lies, which does not match the orders of the lieutenant, who is fighting the real offender, the offensive journalists, who's patrons are mafia another clan, and so on...

"For quite some time the pressing, incisive and objective signals of the press have remained unanswered ..." – Londa seemed to have prophesied this question to her senior teacher.

"While journalists are driven by a genuine desire to improve their lives in any area of public life, the problem identified and raised by it requires a more consistent, systematic, and persistent effort to make readers feel that the publications are effective. Such umbrellas should have received more support from both public and non-governmental organizations. It should be considered intolerable, that when the authorities are less or less responsive to press signals, no one is asked to answer, it is the neglect of the media, which means that publications on the problem will continue indefinitely. Many pressing and pressing issues related to crime and legality await the journalist's pen."

Londa recalled many other conversations with senior colleagues and decided not to interfere with the investigation.

They felt how difficult it was for the journalist profession to sometimes have the right qualifications for a particular story. This proverb should never be used in the country: "Some mud always sticks".

Dudu Arziani entered to the ward quietly.

Londa rolled her eyes at the noise and asked Dudu Arziani:

How did they let you enter?

Dudu, when he heard Londa's voice, rejoiced ... it seemed that he had worse information about her health.

"If you can, tell me what happened?" Dudu asked impatiently.

Londa replied, that she was suddenly attacked by masked men and they demanded for her to get out of the car, as Londa did not obey their orders, she was shot.

"How many were there and where did they meet you?" Dudu asked.

At Ninoshvili street, number 50, near my house. As I recall, there were three people. The only thing, they told to me, was: "We warned you, when we left your Mercedes on bricks. You should stop working on this case, as you did not follow our orders, we can stop it now. They no longer provided me with the answer. As a car was coming from the right side of the yard, they noticed it, fired and fled.

Who called for the emergency car?

It could be the car driver coming out of a neighbor yard.

What's his name, don't you know?

No, I could not see the driver's face, but it was a red Ford car.

I will find out everything in detail and then I will request you again.

Dudu Arziani said good bye to Londa with tenderness and left her room.

Londa was left alone with herself ... She at that time was befriended by a well– known publicist, Natela Onashvili, and kept a keen eye on the public prosecutor she saw. Natela was encouraging her and was increasing her life energy. She was the mother of prosecutor Gigi (Giorgi) Papinashvili, who was killed perfidiously by criminals, and she should know value and strength of words of prosecutor.

Londa remembered "the loud thoughts", the words of City Prosecutor Nikoloz Gabrichidze: "He went out on the balcony, looked over into the city, and suddenly he felt a terrible melancholy ... In front of him was a vivid picture of the current situation, with a thoughtful look at the viciousness of his mother– city, he saw who was trembling with unhealthy vigilance. The obtaining of money was marauding and pillage in city of Tbilisi, once filled with romantic and knightly spirit. Today it would become one endless marketplace, where conscience would be bought most cheaply and readily."

One part of the youth, as if frighten, scared by the flood, was running doomed to flee from the homeland to the radiant world. Yeah, even the guys who had to sail off in a time of bravery, who had to sacrifice themselves to fight in the waves of chaotic conditions like a crippled ship powerlessly rescuing its parent country.

But if, it is truly like Sodom and Gomorrah, the just wrath of God over the whole world for selfishness, stubbornness, has taken place, then where will they take refuge?! Instead of a doomed attempt at personal salvation, it might be better to believe that only Orthodox goodness and mercy would save them and the world tortured by centuries–old famine. However, what hunger for the body has to say, when even a soul devoid of true faith in God is starving. However, nowadays exiled right– wing, captive racketeers, shamefully escaping the scales of law and looking for a reliable backdrop, entertained the unshakable conscience of a dozen honest fellows with his enchanted hands.

In these thoughts, Londa seemed to have a concern that, like Mirza Kurdiani and Nikoloz Gabrichidze, he would kneel down on his own capital and never fall into the trap of a "black" world and for himself and his future prosperity.

NEW WITNESS

Dudu and Koka began investigate of the case. Unfortunately, there were appearing many question marks.

Upon returning to work, they found out that a red Ford on Ninoshvili Street belonged to a former police officer, some David Keburia. This person was fired several months ago as if for allegedly confronting management.

This generally accepted quick information needed verification. it may have been a giver of very important information, evidence.

Dudu was informed, that at Turtle Lake there some

visitor appeared. So, all three investigators recklessly made their way to the lake.

Dudu, Goga, and Koka after consultation shared roles. Under the supervision of the current task force, they had to go into hiding places on both sides. However, the hideout also had a third entrance, which only the operatives knew about.

Dudu and Koka were waiting for twilight to start the planned operation. They had thoroughly studied every corner of the Turtle Lake hiding place. Who could be the "guest"?! – It would probably be from the circle of Jankoteli. After consultation the security guard, it was revealed that security personnel had taken photos of the "guest" of the hideout. However, he was wearing a flamboyant, military–style boots on his feet, and wore a knit hat on his head. He was a tall, skinny of build and was holding two black plastic bags in his hand, and seemed quite confused, as if he was scared. He walked down the slope ...

It was a late evening. There was darkness all around. Only the light of the new moon was dimly visible. The visitor removed a flashlight from his plastic bag and headed directly to the side door of the hideout. It was clear, that he was not there for the first time. He touched his hand underneath the metal door and opened it. He looked around the area with a flashlight and went inside. The door was carefully closed. For a few minutes, there was the sound of a rusted door closing. The guards were watching silently for about 10– 15 minutes. Waiting ... because it was easy for the "visitor" side to spy on them.

There was a long silence. ... The guards were alerting the duty crew about the incident. The key was to get a quick response from the person on duty. The hideout was surrounded on every side. No sound was heard from the "guest". Within an hour the armed group was already fully mobilized. Koka could not wait and tested the door of the hideout, the door from which the "visitor" entered. It door was closed.

Then Koka hid again, watching from afar for his response. Shortly thereafter the wind started blowing. Turtle Lake knows strong winds. This place is known to the locals as the wind zone.

The wind was quite noisy and even if the stone was thrown to the door, Anyone inside would not have understood the wind or the artificially created noise. The hideout had only three small windows, protected only by barbed wire. The "visitor" seemed to be asleep deeply. Dudu pointed the security guard toward the second door. They opened the door easily and sneaked in. The guest in the very first room was really asleep. Before looking at black bag, Dudu decided to create photo materials first. First the room and plastic bag were taken, and then the photo– materials and the Makarov system's ammunition from the plastic bag. Dudu and Koka did not awaken the "visitor" and asked the guards to proceed with inspection and examine with great vigilance.

They wondered who the next "guest" would be, or what the person would do. Investigators and the task force were waken and waiting until the morning. They couldn't even feel their hands from the cold. They were dreaming about hot tea and the warm fireplace. Each was in anticipation of new "guests." In the meantime, they heard some noise from the hiding place, the "visitor", who was sleeping all night long, was waking up and talking on the phone or, on the radio it was unclear. The words were not heard clearly, only repeated three times that there was peace. An hour after this conversation, everything around was still silent, but still the unbearable wind buzzing was heard.

The investigators waited in vain for the rest of the "guests" ... but they did not appear. It was time for action. The decision was made and even fulfilled. The person, visitor was arrested, and was searched at the time of his arrest, he did not have an ID, but instead of ID was found a pocketbook containing a "Yard keepers" book, which failed to identify his identity, as it was discoloured.

AKHALKATSI OR NAVROZASHVILI?

Investigators opened the package and what they saw, was Photographs of Londa, taken in different circumstances. In particular, the moment she left home, the very day that the mobs attacked her. Londa wore a pink T– shirt and her glasses matched the description also. That is, the photos were taken on the day of the attack ... they were pretty much all over the desk. There were also photos of the day Londa's car was left on the bricks. Dudu looked closely at a photograph of Londa's car, it was dark, but you could see faintly a man's face. It was difficult to identify with the naked eye. Goga looked through all the photos, including photos of the Londa's family ... Every move was recorded and they decided to get expert examination for a thorough examination of the photo material, and at the same time to determine the origin of the camera. Since the camera didn't look like a lover's camera, it was more professional, almost like criminals being accounted for. Without it, no one can have access.

In addition, the photos showed almost all of Londa's actions, taken in the yard of Solomon Kalandadze. She was barely recognized by members of the group, as on the day Solomon met, Londa was dressed in an unobtrusive, old–fashioned Adidas sports outfit, sporting a knit hat.

On the photographs were also identified Ucha and Mirian, dressed in a special outfit, having conversation with Sergi Menabde. What is the connection between the turtle lake hideout and Solomon Kalandadze's yard? Why did they take these photos in hiding and who should receive them and why? – After all, Dudu was thinking seriously about Londa's security and he had a real fear.

He remembered that Londa was right, when she felt a great danger ... So, why was her home address changed?! Why did she move from Ortachala to Ninoshvili? She used to live in an isolated apartment? – and, perhaps, she did not feel safe there. Here, on Ninoshvili, there is an Italian yard with her old neighbours living like one family, she felt more secure. Precious people, who respected her very much and looked after her... One of them even often washed her car in the common yard, and the another one, neighbouring woman, would look after her children, preparing them dinner too. Londa was pleasantly surprised as well as grateful. But she was even more surprised, when she learned that in their yard, so called the "law thief" lived.

"A prosecutor and a thief in the same yard?"– Dudu recalled Londa's words ... He knew about this matter, how she was worrying about it and was looking for a way out of this situation.

Dudu suddenly imagined Londa's children, delightfully player in their yard, and decided to focus on them first, as they could be in danger.

INTERROGATION OF THE "GUEST" AT THE PROSECUTOR GENERAL'S OFFICE

After acknowledging the photos and ammunition, the quantity of bullets and shells from to the investigative team numerous questions arose. Only the "guest", whose real name was not yet known for investigation, would answer the questions. The questioning was conducted by Dudu Arziani:

Tell us your last name and first name. – Mamuka Akhalkatsi.

The year and place of birth. – 1972, Gori.

Dwelling place?

I have no apartment. I live with relatives. I'm not at the same address.

Whatever you said, tell us all the addresses, where you spent nights.

I don't know the addresses, I can take you there and show them you.

Surnames and names?

Sergy Menabde, Gizo Khomeriki and Zaza Khuluzauri. – Can you show us Zaza Khuluzauri's house?

of course.

Do you know Where is he currently? – I cannot tell you.

How do you know these people?

From the office.

Where's Sergi Menabde? – Sergy is in the hospital.

Why he is in the hospital?

He was wounded in the prison cell. – Did he injure himself?

No, the prisoners probably wounded him.

How do you know that the prisoners wounded him? – Well, I was a prisoner too.

Do you have this information from prison?

My sister, Lia Navrozashvili informed me also. – How does your sister have this information?

My sister works as a nurse at the hospital where Sergi resides. – And you want to say that you have this information from Sergi

Menabde?

Well, I can't tell you. Why are you asking me?

However, Menabde can't talk, since the day he was wounded and was hospitalized, how do you explain that?

I don't know why you ask me?

What do you pay for your sentence?

This question made Akhalkatsi completely confused. – Is your sister on her spouse's last name?

Akhalkatsi became silent and thought to avoid the question. – She is not married.

well! you are Navrozashvili as well and don't want to admit about it.

After a little silence, Akhalkatsi admitted that he was indeed serving a suspended sentence and it was Mamuka Navrozashvili, not Mamuka Akhalkatsi.

Well, this book is so damaged, cannot be read clearly, but in spite of it, there is not written Navrozashvili. – There is written Mamuka Akhalkatsi.

What Surname is written in the proof of identity?

Mamuka Akhalkatsi is written but I think I really lost it. – Where do you keep your documents?

I have no documents.

What kind relationship do you have with Khomeriki?

I am friend with his brother, we were sitting together on the first sentence.

Where is he now?

He is on sentence again, for attempted assassination.

Do you know who he wanted to kill?

No, I know that he was blamed, or rather he took it upon himself.

Who wanted him to kill, tell us.

If you have heard about "scissors" ... He is sitting instead of him.

Does Scissors know that he's lying?

He is sitting there because of "scissors." – Do you know Scissors?

No, but I heard about him being a "law thief," "working" in Russia, not here.

Well, but didn't you say just now because of him, he was sentenced?

But "Scissors" paid big money to Gizo Khomeriki's brother and he took himself blaming of Suliko Jankhoteli.

However, please, do not make this information public, otherwise they will kill me.

Why were you charged? still because of them?

Suliko's brother, who is a police officer, killed a man accidently, and I was sentenced for him.

Did they pay you for it? – –No, they scared me ...

How? why? did you have some secret?

I had some debt with Menabde and he asked me to do it for that reason.

These clothe you are wearing, where did you buy it? – I haven't bought it, they gave me.

Who gave you it if it's not a secret? – One guy, he is a military person.

What's his name, don't you know?

No, he's dating Jankhoteli, Jaba is his name, I don't know his last name.

Have you heard about the high– profile case of the murder of prosecutor Mirza Kurdiani?

I know a little something.

What do you know, tell us the truth and stay with us.

I have got my freedom with great difficulty and I don't want lose it. I don't want to go back.

Suddenly Koka stepped in and demanded attendance, which Dudu agreed to.

"You're two now and I can't tell you," – Navrozashvili hesitated. – By the way, the words of two men are stronger, for heaven's sake, we do not really want to catch you and return you to prison. tell us the truth, and you will always be with us, next to us.

I know, that they were scaring a decent man.

How did they do it in the country protected by laws?

I know that they paid big money to him and he was sent to abroad after the murder.

What are you saying, don't you know his exact last name and where he was sent?

I know, that he was the military once, he sent to me two pairs of boots as a gift. He knew I was, theirs.

You have just now said, that "they" scared you also, who do you talk about and who do you mean in "they?"

When the crime took place, then they asked me about "help". – what do you mean?

I sent the explosives to the Menabde by Aziza's hand. – But, you were in jail, didn't you say now?

Yes, it is true, and with the help of my sister, I was sentenced to probation and was freed three months before.

Has your sister any influence on them? – Koka asked. – She is their slave, they scare her.

How are they scaring her? Or perhaps they respect her, what does the "fear" mean?

I will tell you the truth, my sister is used and they force her to do their work.

Tell us one specific thing they did, and it will help your sister. – I want Sergi to survive now, but my sister is scared and, as I know from my sister, she is forced not to give the drugs to Sergi, which are prescribed for him.

I know that my sister had given the forbidden tablets twice to Sergi silently... and that morning Sergi opened his eyes, and for this my sister had problems with those people.

Do you want to save Sergi?

No, I don't really want him to die, but, I know, as soon as he is better, he will denounce about me, give away me.

You sat with Sergi?

Yes, we were sitting in one cell.

And you were ordered to kill Sergi? After a long silence:

I had this assignment from those guys.

If you did not comply, were you threatened? – Yes, I would be in Sergi's situation now.

Did the prison supervisors know about this? – The one knew, they called him as"Fourers". – How, was this negotiation with you?

Yes, it was decided when we met.

Where did the negotiations take place? – In prison, in the interrogation room.

Did the negotiations take place outside the prison too? – Yes, at Suliko Jankhotel's casino.

How many people were at his negotiation?

I was not present there, I was in jail at the time and I can't tell you exactly.

Who came to you?

Investigator, I do not remember his surname, and he handed me a "greetings" from Gaga Jankhoteli and "Scissors".

How did you know that the prison supervisor knew about it? – He was open with me and was telling me everything.

Well, how did the prosecutor get killed and why, do you know about it?

The prosecutor was killed in his own yard.

Who was the killer, maybe you can remember the name?

I know the name, I already told it you, "Boots" gave me, military "Boots" – two pairs. Jaba is his name. Tall and skinny young man, with blond hair and blue eyes, with a deep voice.

Why did he kill him?

I told you, it was ordered by "Scissors" and a police chief. I don't really know the police officer's last name.

An weapon? What weapon was he killed with? Do you know?

I don't know. I don't know much.

Was the killer alone?

Yes, he was alone.

Were you also offered this job?

No, but there is always doubt about me.

Isn't Jaba suspicious?

No, at the same time, Suliko made Jaba to lose big money in the casino and he was becoming deprived man, to repay his debt he had to sell his house.

Sum, don't you know how much it was?

15,000 USD, thus he was losing both, job and his family.

And, was this divine man killed for $ 15,000?

What can I tell you, I didn't like this story.

What did you do on the lake?

I cannot say... they will kill me.

Well, then tell us why you wanted photos of Londa Amilakhvari, or her family?

Londa is ruthless, she was warned several times, given some sign to be stopped, anonymously. Once her car tires were lifted and bricks laid, and the other times she was threatened to kill her children.

How do you know all these, who told you all about it?

Engaged in angry Arziani.

I was personally asked to do this. – How? did you shoot her?

Yes, I shot, but I could not kill her, felt sorry for her and wounded just in her shoulder.

What task did you have? to kill her? – Yes, they were getting rid of her.

In particular, who gave the order to you?

I was ordered by the "Scissors", but I cannot sin, he had a difficulty to ask me it.

So, you couldn't make a request?

Yes, I have a new assignment, as you can see, it's a tool that killed the prosecutor ... and I have photos of all the members of her family.

How do you know that it is that weapon?

Well, I was told that this gun would only kill prosecutors. Of course, they were joking, but in this joke I realized that it was Mirza Kurdian's murder weapon.

Go back to the hideout, whose order was that you stayed there? – No, they don't trust this secret hideous anymore. I went on my own initiative there, I told you, I live with my sister and she's checking around me everything all the time, and I know she is in friendly relationship with Londa and she won't betray her. So that, I went to the hideout.

This time, the interrogation is over. Dudu and I decided, to let you go free for now. But you must know that your every movement is under control. You must cooperate with the investigation and neither you nor your sister won't be hurt. When we need it, you will be called and equipped accordingly. What concerns your coat, it is sent down to the exit, put it on there and go. But wear it always, to recognise you easily everywhere. Your costume is in another room. You can get dressed and wear it too. You won't be recognise otherwise. Be there in Turtle Lake hideous and summon, call the people there. Your security is determined by your involvement in the case.

Mamuka Akhalkatsi (Navrozashvili) was seen off as far as the first corner by Dudu and Koka and the phones were exchanged amicably. They were pleased with the results of the interrogation, secretly outfitting his clothe and jacket with bugging devises.

The danger of destroying Londa was real. So, she was discharged from the hospital and continued treatment in the operative hide. Consequently, her children were also hidden until the end of the next operation.

WAS HE INSANE?

The juvenile, accused Aziz Muradov, has finally been fixed judicially – psychiatric examination and was diagnosed that since he's been nine years of age, attempted several times to commit suicide, had auditory and visual hallucinations and, therefore, hence it follows that his mental state, the time of commitment of crime Aziz Muradov could not beheld responsible for his actions. According to which diagnosis the defendant needed inpatient psychiatric care. Londa, who was in hiding, felt rather weak. The physicians' consortium decided to continue her treatment at its rehabilitation center. She didn't even want to hear that, as she had plenty of jobs to do. In particular, she was deeply concerned about the spiritual condition of that suspicious minor. That was why she did not think of much, she called a taxi and went to work.

Londa was frightened by the inadequate and impulsive behavior of juvenile Aziz Muradov. At times, she doubted if someone was encouraging him, to behave like that to play as if being sick. Londa called the group to discuss the case of Aziz Muradov. First, it was necessary for the two investigators to enter Aziz's investigative detention facility to find out the legal status of the accused how he was treated by the prison administration.

Londa wanted to become sure that the expert's report was perfect and, therefore, new questions arose.

Was he abusive at the time of the crime, had he had limited confession? Did the situation worsen after his arrest? Because the expert unambiguously found that he is offensive in dynamics. Londa decided to turn to the expert for further questions:

1. Did the defendant have a temporary mental disorder at that time?
2. Was he suffering from chronic mental illness at the time of the crime?
3. Whether he could give a proper testimony because of his mental state.

Londa was worrying about the case because: Sergi Menabde was still in serious condition, Suliko Jankhoteli was wounded in the head, and accused Aziz Muradov was ill with irreparable mental problems.

The first thing that needed to be done was that Aziz Muradov would have rushed from prison for treatment. Londa also wondered why the inpatient psychiatrist had not recommended him to the patient's treatment and why he had been remanded to a correctional facility.

The next morning, investigators approached Aziz Muradov at the scheduled time. The prison controller, for some reason, did not appear for a long time, and the prison staff **suspiciously** were running up and down in the stairs. Koka asked what the movements were and why? Appeared, that Aziz Muradov was found to be strangling his cellmate and the situation had hardly subsided. Instead of being taken to the penitentiary, the prison administration transferred him to an isolated cell. The abusive inmate was punished for his inadequate behavior. The result has been horrific ...

The accused Aziz Muradov hung himself.

This was an unprecedented case, as none of the sections showed any prejudice, failed to comply with the law, and this indifference endowed claimed the life of a minor.

WHO IS RESPONSIBLE FOR THE CRIME?

Londa convened a meeting to discuss three issues:

1. Examine practices that controlled the next stage of the established mental diagnosis and, generally, was it controlled or not.
2. Who was in charge of monitoring the behaviors of a sick prisoner – the escort or the chief physician? or both sides together?
3. Should it be the norm to transfer a mentally ill inmate from the forensic ward directly to the ward of the psychiatric hospital?

These questions should be answered by the competent authorities. Namely, the head of the National Forensics Bureau and the penitentiary institution.

Does the offender need special treatment and appropriate conditions? The aforementioned workers should be well–versed in these matters, as neglecting this factor may endanger other prisoners. The prisoner's psyche is already disrupted by the deprivation of liberty and minor misconduct can lead to fateful consequences. In this particular case, this is what happened to Aziz Muradov. Once the abuser was identified within his competence, he needed to be prescribed medication that was neither for others nor for himself. The rights of the ailing prisoner were clearly violated, and Aziz Muradov, an accomplice in the offensive, fell into the hands of his companion. He almost became a killer of his cellmate.

It was also a crime that his companions were not aware of his abuse, otherwise they would be cautious. And, even the worse than everything was it that in result of this mistake, he hung himself.

This was prompted by people who locked him in an isolated cell alone. Why was it not understood before entering the cell how lawful and permissible it was to allow the inmate to be brought from a mental hospital to a normal cell, or so– called Putting him in jail? It is not a wonder, that a sick teenager who stays isolated hangs himself!

In these thoughts, Londa was looking for a way out of the situation. Absolute caution was needed in the case.

Thousands of small thinks are found in everyday practice. If all of us were to pay attention and not face such problems indifferently, such a thing would never happen. These is all about the fate of people here... to the children of your country, who have committed a crime but are serving their sentences. Why do you make life difficult for people, who are already punished and spend most of their lives in prison walls?

CITY HOSPITAL

On Monday morning in the City Hospital, where Sergi Menabde was hospitalized, doctors were taking turns on a newly arrived shift and it was almost replaced by new staff. The only person, who was left out of the old footage, was Lia Navrozashvili, who was diligently putting in the new shift. She was thoroughly aware of each patient and loved her job, but she was subjected to intimidation from those with criminal activities. Vepkhia Lomidze knew the price of Lia's devotion. Though, he was warned as the chief doctor to take immediate action to release her, but he only managed to write a statement on her vacation. This factor eliminated the mistrust that the Security Service had with Lia Navrozashvili once.

Sergi Menabde was moved from the city hospital to the prison resuscitation unit. As soon as he became better, he immediately requested a meeting with Londa Amilakhwari. He was told about the attack on Londa, but he didn't want to talk to anyone except Londa, as he trusted just her.

Londa went to work. She was advised to go to rehab, but she stubbornly wanted to continue the investigation of the case ... and she did it. She was preparing to meet with Sergi Menabde, and she once again had a interview with her bosses about this issue. The meeting unanimously decided to interrogate Sergi Menabde.

PENITENTIARY HOSPITAL

Londa Amilakhwari obtained the permission to interrogate the accused Sergi Menabde from chief physician, Naolis Kobulia. Mr. Naolis was a strong specialist in the field of surgery. In the presence of a physician, he allowed Londa to interrogate the patient and warned her that all questions should be handled with great professional caution and the patient should not be overtired. The interrogation deadline was set – a maximum of one hour.

Londa began the questioning:

If you remember, what happened on the night of the accident? – I remember almost all the details.

Have you had any arguments with your cellmates?

Many peculiar people were in our cell. As I mentioned in previous testimonies. Azeris, Armenians and Russians were also in the cell with Georgians. The previous evening, another inmate, Mamuka Akhalkatsi, was brought to my cell. I noticed that he was quite nervous. I was trying to get somehow used to the locked space and talk. He replied: "My brother, your trying in vain to calm me down. I am an innocent man. On the contrary, they wanted to kill me and here I was arrested." His words sounded so sincere, I believed that he was innocent. Mamuka was put on the first tier. However, there was only a place on the second tier. Azer was asked to exchange a place, and he also agreed.

Was there any deal with Azeri?

It is possible, because only he was watching my wounding and, as I felt, he knew.

What do you think, if the killer needed his help, would he do it?

How, was not it a help to be kept silence when the killer was killing me?

And more, I remember the aggression of the Azeri prisoner at the previous days towards me. Unfortunately, I made the conclusion later about it.

Now, exactly remember, how did Akhalkatsi deal with you, on which tier did you then lie?

I was lying on the first tier, Mamuka suggested drinking water and he also checked, if I was awake and offered me also the water. I pretended to be asleep, as I felt somehow in danger. I learned from Mamuka that he was more skilled than me. This time he was doing some ordered tasks.

Checking me once again, he whispered into my ear: "Are you asleep"?

I still did not answer him, after which I had two wounds to my head and chest. I couldn't even shout or call for any help, it happened so fast and I passed out, unconscious.

Did you feel aggression from the other cell fellows?

–By the way, I am not angel either.

How was the aggression expressed and by whom?

We were all aggressive.

And why were you?

I was asked a lot of questions that they couldn't receive answers and they were aggressive.

Everything is clear about the cell. Do you remember anything from the hospital situation? Or did you hear the conversations periodically?

I heard it twice, they were talking about me, that I would not survive.

Who were they specifically, do you remember it, or what was the tone of it?

The voice of the woman was as if familiar, but I can't remember, who she should have been. She was talking to a man, unfamiliar to me.

Are you aware of Lia Navrozashvili?

Yes, I know, but I can't remember where I know from. However, I remembered about her, she is a sister or cousin of my cellmate.

How did you know Mamuka before?

From afar, he was in friendship with a police officer, Jankhoteli, and his brother.

When they settled him in the cell, did you greet each other?

Yes, of course. Mamuka expressed more affection towards me. – How do you think, why he wanted to kill you?

He was probably instructed and he was performing. – Did not they trust you?

No, they did not, as they were as one family, they would never open me fully their secrets. I was just as a blind weapon for them, but Mamuka Akhalkatsi was close to them and they considered him almighty.

Who you include when you say "they"? You mention them in the plural and whom do you call the "others"?

Sergi Menabde became nervous, anxious, it was difficult to say names. Londa explained, told him her situation, she also reminded him, how he was warning and asking her, to be careful. This information led Sergi out of the situation and named the criminals.

Londa, if not you, I might would not be alive anymore. I have no right to be silent. These are Gizo Khomeriki, Zaza Khuluzauri, scissors, brothers Jankhotelis, Mamuka and Lia Akhalkatsi.

Are you aware that the person named Lia was your nurse at the hospital?

I just now realized it, I had never seen her in the hospital, I just recognised her voice.

In the meantime, an hour had passed, and Naulis Kobulia reminded the investigator of her time. Londa was unable to interview Sergi anymore and gave him time to recover.

THE MAIN WITNESS WAS SUMMONED TO THE PROSECUTOR'S OFFICE

The Prosecutor General of Georgia convened a meeting, which unanimously decided that witness Solomon Kalandadze and his family should be questioned. Mirza Kurdiani's neighbours: Rusudan Mikaia and the hostage of the criminals, mother of four, were also to be questioned as witnesses.

Procedural instructions were passed to prosecutors, Gocha Tsamaladze and Nana Cherkezia. This assignment was planned within the purview of absolute competence, making it impossible for Londa to appear at this stage, since, as the Witnesses knew her personally.

A group of prosecutors, temporarily set up at the prosecutor's office, has started working. Initially it was decided to interview Londa Amilakhwari.

Londa was pleased with herself, she had the ultimate goal of winning. She had to temporarily give up her position, as the case demanded. She was fully aware of the situation and had met Solomon. Londa met with the new staff of prosecutors, they went through all the details and decided to continue her relationship with Suliko Jankhoteli, and the new group had to comply with the decision made by the Prosecutor General.

Prosecutors: Gocha Tsamaladze and Nana Cherkezia were preparing to meet the witness in the morning. The first postmaster informed them that Solomon Kalandadze was in the reception room. The new group provided security for the witness's prosecution as mothers in black rallied in the reception area and demanded a meeting with the prosecutor general. Solomon was raised, taken up silently in this mess. Gocha Tsamaladze started questioning:

To the first question whether he knew Mirza Kurdiani, he immediately replied that he knew him from afar because Mirza was avoiding active contacts with his neighbours.

What do you know about Mirza Kurdiani's murder? – Mirza Kurdiani was killed near his entrance.

Where from do you have this information?

"From the neighbours," Solomon replied confused. Where were you on the night of the murder?

At work.

Where did you work?

I worked as an engineer in a footwear factory.

Did you go to work every day and work on the same schedule?

No, how can I tell you? the orders with us was generally messed up, but I couldn't get home until two o'clock in the morning, as I was head of the factory.

Do you want to say that you were at work from 9am to 2pm? – Well, sir, we were helping the war guys, we were making military shoes and sending them.

Do you explain the style of the shoes?

We were called "Batinka", so called high– heeled boots. – Have you got these shoes for sale?

No, these shoes would not be sold, we were only caring for those involved in the war. So we warned the staff strongly, as we lacked material and therefore our products had to be shipped carefully.

Did you ever noticed you shoes on any other person, on ordinary citizens, not on soldiers.

Solomon Kalandadze remembered that the killer was wearing shoes from his factory and realized that the prosecution had information. He was referring to an anonymous card he had written, which said "Batinka" and decided to tell the truth:

I will tell you about the murder, but the leverage of protecting me and my family is gone. I know they are watching me.

How do you know?

I was warned on the home phone, they threatened me.

Who was specifically, do you remember the sound, or the specific words?

I'm ashamed to repeat it, but it was a woman who warned me not to say anything even in my own family.

Did she called you just once?

No, it happened several times. The threat was in one text that I would not live, if I revealed this secret. The lady asked me to keep our conversations a secret, that she knew and respected me, that she was my wife's colleague and for this reason she was warning me.

Have you ever thought about changing your address?

How? No such thing happens silently. Wherever I go,

they will find me everywhere. Until the killer is identified and detained, serious threats are to be expected.

Who lives in your neighborhood?

Which particular neighbour do you mean? – Your neighbour next door.

Russiko Mikaia lives.

What kind is your relationship with Mikaia?

Normal. The Mrs is the chair of the apartment and therefore we have a business relationship with her.

What is your dog's name?

It is black bulldog, with white heart and its name is "Chichi". – We heard that "Chichi" was shot in the entrance with a gun...

Who wounded it and why?

I think it was a warning wound, they threatened me with it I think so.

Did anyone meet you on the subject of murder?

Solomon became thoughtful and asked to go outside and to smoke. Ms. Nana Cherkezia allowed him to smoke in her room and continued with the interrogation:

Did they made any promises in return for your silence?

Well, it was so, and they offered great sums, but I promised to keep the secret without money. I have no relationship with them, and neither can I.

If you remember, where were you from the morning of the murder to the evening and what were you doing?

Of course, I remember everything ... I left home a little early that morning, had a lot of work. It was Wednesday as long as I can remember. My job is in Isani district. Since the war as we have there a shortage of transport, so I was leaving early, at 12 pm. I was getting home from work at two o'clock at night. I had to walk in the front of at the building, where Mr. Mirza Kurdiani lived.

Suddenly, a white "Volga" stopped and Mr. Mirza got out. I looked at the car number – 32– 13 and it was his car. It was late, and it was dark, the street lights were not working. Mr Mirza's lights were on, and it was against this background, that a young man approached him and fired several bullets. It happened in front of me, I saw everything with my own eyes. The killer turned around and disappeared. before he turned, I was standing front of him face to face, so I remember him well. I am still surprised, at how I was kept alive. I could have been killed to erase a trace, but he didn't do it. The gun was shot, but it was not fired. That's, how I survived that night... But Mr. Mirza died on the spot.

Please, describe in detail the appearance and attire of the killer?

It would have been 185 centimeters, lean and emaciated, with straight nose, a black woven hat on his head, a brown jacket, and on the feet I know exactly that he was wearing my factory, our military boots.

What do you think, did he look like a military man?

If we take into consideration of his guts and deliberate actions, and the fact that he was wearing the boots for military personnel, I think, 90 percent that he is a military man.

Did not the neighbours make noises? Did they come out?

Yes, they did, but I suddenly went home. It is possible, that my neighbour Rusudan Mikaia saw me. As I heard the sound of her door closing.

It is enough at this point. We will protect your safety. You have to keep silent.

Solomon was shown out through a side door, so that, he would not be seen by anyone.

ALI TARKHUN'S SEASIDE VILLA

According to recent reports, Gizo Khomeriki was hiding in Samsung with his accomplice. He was visiting a former military pilot and now arms dealer Ali Tarkhun. Gizo Khomeriki met Ali Tarkhun during the military training and became to him so close that they visited each other at least twice a year. Ali had a beautiful sister Javidan, working as a Chief Physician of Samsun Hospital. She was not married and engaged in ascetic life.

Gizo Khomeriki was very fond of blue eyed Javidan. He had a feeling, that Javidan would have Georgian ancestors. He did not dare to talk with her about this matter, but he definitely had doubt about it. Gizo used to go to his warehouse every day, where he had a secret room and worked there from morning to evening. He was making jack knives and daggers. In that warehouse, criminals would gather and sort out the various situations. Who would have thought that Gizo Khomeriki, a military man, would have been involved in criminal activity, and it would have given him great pleasure. Who wouldn't see you here... They were visiting as Turkish traitors, as weapons' specialists coming from different countries.

Ali had a small villa at the seaside, where he was hosting drug dealers and gunmen from neighbouring countries. There was a wall of sandstone around the villa. The peacocks walked in the garden amongst Cinderella and clover flowers, and in the corner, in an iron cage, a lion was kept. The back-yard was planted with forest trees. There were Doberman dogs tied on long wire in the yard. The trail was going from the villa down to the seashore, where was moored two motorboats.

One night Gizo stayed alone in the villa. The smell of the sea and the sound of waves was like the sound of his parent praying for him. He remembered his childhood. He grew up in Gagra and spent many fortunate years on the Bzif River. He had feeling, as he was in Gagra, as Samsong somehow resembled his Gagra, like the blue– eyed Javidian resembled to Georgian woman. He remembered his studies ... He graduated from the Sokhumi Institute of Subtropics and could not get a job because of the war. He was wounded three times and escaped from obvious death. He became so nervous that he was unable to control himself. The biggest spiritual trauma he experienced when his young mother and father were shot by the Abkhazians in the war, then he was 23 years old. He would since then walk the path of life alone, quietly and proudly. Gizo always remembered Indian's saying that: "Peace is a state where there are only objective thoughts and desires inside you." He seemed to be following in the right footsteps of his ancestors, but where and when did he miss his aims and make him turn away? When and what made him change his righteous thoughts and the same time lose his peace of mind? He practically was like a lost ship without any fuel, desperately sinking in the middle of the sea, with its passengers missing the sign of life and only one fleeting hopelessly driven, perhaps miraculously escaping from obvious death of the murky waves of the sea, all hopes lost already. Unfortunately, such a situation reveals a diminished man, who has forgotten the moral standards of his survival and he signs up for all immorality. For example, on guns, drugs ... and who knows, the lost ship, which takes its passengers, which shore on it will hit. So is a man on his lost way. Result? – The result is really fatal ... because to remain as a man in this transient world, is a great heroism. And here is the defeat caused by his own criminal passions ... Unfortunately, Gizo Khomeriki's mental portrait could never guarantee that he would not commit a crime again. However, once he meditated deeply on his worthless conduct, he even tried to kill himself. It is a spiritual pathology, it is depression, and it is a sick state of the organism body, that manifests itself in spiritual agony. Suicide is studied by Suicideology and it is a world problem. where there is a lack of human life development related to the difficult social situation, and the spread of this dangerous event in Georgia was very large. Gizo Khomeriki's life appeared exactly in this condition, he was now surviving, but unfortunately, his life was vain and wasted, without any honour. Gizo Khomeriki fell asleep in sweet– bitter memories. In his dream, he was seeing the Turkish beautiful woman, who looked very much like a Georgian ...

VISITORS TO ALI TARKHUN

In the morning, Gizo Khomeriki was awakened by the chanting of nightingales. Thinking in a dream, and wishing to pursue this pleasure with another pleasure, he repeatedly telephoned Javidan, who answered Gizo with usual pride, but the voice clearly showed warmth and tenderness to him. She said, that there were arrived the guests from Tbilisi. Gizo was waiting for them. He was experiencing a lack of information. So it was necessary to meet with same, like–minded people.

Amongst then, he was scared just of "Scissors", as he was an unpredictable man, and no one knew what he was going to do, what could be in his mind. To the others, Zaza Khuluzauri and some Gogicha he did not have any fear.

The men brought four ammunition and three hunting weapons. Khomeriki was amazed at how they were able to get the weapons through the border controls without troubles. Scissors kept silent, and Zaza Khuluzauri questened Gizo Khomeriki:

What kind host is Ali Tarkhun, does it forces you something unusual? or scares you?

No, on the contrary, Ali is a true friend, but he demands great prices in arms.

What about narcotics?

He is a drug addict, but we have to have a different attitude towards drugs.

Did you start a new workshop? As I recall, some details were missing.

I do not know, I have not seen a new workshop...And, what is a workshop for?

For weapon production.

Is the old factory still there?

Well, maybe the old one will be delivered, given to us. After a little silence, Gizo reluctantly asked:

What kind girl is Javidan?

In response to this question, "Scissors" surprisingly asked: – Do you like her?

No, but she's such a good woman.

Don't make a mistake, she's as a family member, you know? – Well, I only asked, what and why should I do bad for her?

You have a wife? No, none.

Know, if you think something, you will have to admit it, or leave her.

I don't know yet her well and how can I married her?

I warn you, brother, so cool woman, if you marry her, our brotherhood will grow stronger.

Our brotherhood is already solid. – I mean Ali's and our brotherhood. – I understand.

Ali Tarkhun invited Georgian friends to his family. He covered a large table with half Turkish and half Georgian dishes. On the balcony that was overlooking the sea side, the host was frying the sturgeon barbeque. Gizo grabbed its aroma, he was fascinated by the fish and was eager to get out on the balcony.

Gizo Khomeriki quite long time was on the balcony. Some power struggled him to get to Georgia and to respond there to justice. He was obsessed by disappointment; He realized that he was on a dirty path. His parents would not really like his aim and would stop him. After their deaths, he became helpless before the demon. Getting close to such people at first was frightening and he thought that he would help them to find right way, would recruit and would turn them to the right way, but this terrible circle was poisoned. They had an easy opportunity to earn money and felt a different kind of power. He lost his real family in the war and found himself weak in life. Disillusioned, homeless and unfriendly, he took refuge in a new mafia family. Initially, this family did not trust him and made him thousands of abominations that he was unable to manage it or did badly. For a time, he became suspicious and they even wanted to get rid of him, but Gizo was a clever gifted man, his family's nobility had long prevented him from taking these steps, but ... unfortunately, that bad day arrived, when his life was completely changed. The mother – church was also forgotten, and with it, everything round him was changed.

The only thing that was difficult to do, was ordering of the murder of Mirza Kurdiani, where he would pay his own money. Why, he couldn't explain it. Why did a military person need to kill a prosecutor? Fear– filled task was fulfilled Thieves in law ... he was already in that capacity. He knew, however, that the "thief in law" would never become one, as he had spent years under military uniform.

But they were using him only and, unfortunately, had no other value. So they did not trust to the end. He was stuck somewhere in middle neither on land nor in the sky" ... but Gizo let everything go by just because he liked this blue–eyed woman. However, even would trust him or not, – as he was "the sheep wrapped in wolf's leather. There was a high probability that he would be rejected from Javidan.

However, it is said that "love made crazy Tariel also" and decided to learn Turkish language through a dictionary. So, he could explain now his feelings to Javidan in her own language.

Gizo as if sobered from his thoughts, he stared to the infinite expanse of sea ... as if he was waiting for answers for his questions...and, oh, it was wondering!

"What are you doing alone here, are you in love?" – it was said in Turkish language, and it was said by Javidan's voice.

It seemed so, that his faith had returned to Gizo, thinking that it was already a response from heaven he had abandoned once.

LOVE OF TURKISH GIRL

Ali Tarkhun has been working since morning. He gave a complete description of the weapons that had been prepared for six months to send to Georgia. He was intent on doing his favourite thing. He liked Georgian brothers, but could not communicate with them without an interpreter. They had an interpreter, a Georgian Turk, who could hardly say in old Lazarus or broken Georgian. But after Gizo learned Turkish, the translator was no longer hired. Gizo was completely satisfied with this role, because without him there was no word, and he was translating, how he liked it.

Ali Bey was a believer in the man speaking his native language more than the others.

As soon as Gizo woke up, he found Ali Bay and started talking with him. Ali, as if swallowing his tongue, did not answer him. He was doing his work quietly. In the meantime, Gizo has begun to look at Ali Bay's books. One of the books he found a photo of Javidan. He took the photograph and hid into his heart pocket and continued to look around the closet. A glossy Georgian dictionary on the third shelf in the closet, attracted him. Gizo immediately took it and started turning the pages. On the first page with distorted Georgian letters was scribbled: Javidan Tarkhun... "So, what does it mean? Javidian is learning Georgian"? – Gizo was astonished. It also seems clear that she has just begun to learn the language ... may it's because of me? Is it love? No, what a nonsense, she doesn't know me well, does she know Georgian and has she heard my phone conversations? Then she knows that I am in love.

From these thoughts the voice of Javidan revealed, she asked him in Georgian:

Have you examined all the books? – Yes, almost.

Which one did you choose to read? – none!

Why?

Because I want to read for you them.

It will be difficult. I do not recommend.

Let's see. – answered the astonished surprised Gizo and asked only one question to Javidan: – Have your ancestors been Georgians in the past?

Yes, they were Georgians and they were Pataridze. We couldn't keep up the surname because of the historical misfortune, otherwise I'm a Turkish in Georgia and Georgian in Turkey and I love both the same way, like I love my Nenei and Babai.

Gizo felt proud ... imagining himself as a genius, because he had no doubt that this family had something to do with Georgia. He always thought that it was not a Turkish but a Georgian Javidan ... but it did not matter to him what nationality his beloved lady was... because in reality he fell in love with a very virtuous Turkish girl. That was, probably, the irony of fate, because he did not know, what his fate will bring him in future, how would develop his life. Will he lose her too because of his dark past? However, depending on his way of life, he realized that, he won't be granted from his fate nothing divine, as in his body lives Demon and never gives him possibility to enjoy with a normal life. He is a killer, and will be in endless fights with his conscience. Though, because of his sins, he can never get any forgiveness.

Suddenly, the sound of the police sirens deafened the seaside. Turkish police besiege Ali Tarkhun's palace. They demanded from the criminals to be surrendered peacefully, without any resistance. This requirement has been repeated several times in Turkish and Georgian languages.Ali Tarkhun handed Gizo a gun. Gogicha, "Scissors" and Zaza escaped from the room and armed themselves with machine guns.

Javidan was not to be seen anywhere, she had disappeared. Scissors launched his machine gun into the air, declaring war

with the police. Ali Bey urged Gizo to come to the underground exit. However, he repeatedly demanded from them to go into the hiding place, in order not to be questioned by the police. "Scissors" ran downstairs, and Ali followed him to show them a secret way. They were going with shooting to the exit. Police surrounded the palace with a live fence and again called for peaceful surrender.

Suddenly, Javidan voice was heard, she was crying... Gizo looked out from the balcony and saw handcuffed Javidan.

He was shocked to see this, and promised the police that if Javidan would be released, he would give himself up, he would surrender. The police uncuffed Javidan after a short silence. Gizo asked for forgiveness in Turkish, and Javidani thanked him in Georgian.

Gizo Khomeriki was arrested.

The police quickly followed in the footsteps of the other criminals, keeping the door open.

Soon the gunshots were heard ...

In three hours' time, four bodies, including Ali Bay's, were transported to the Samsung Hospital's prosectorium. Gizo Khomeriki surrendered to Turkish policemen, because of Javidan love and self– sacrifice. Thus, for this reason his life was preserved and saved.

THE WANTED GIZO KHOMERIKI WAS HANDED OVER TO THE GEORGIAN SIDE

Attorneys, Zaal Rostiashvili and Mikheil Nozadze, arrived at Tbilisi Police Detention Center. The detainee's first request was to find out the whereabouts of a Turkish citizen Javidan Tarkhun. Gizo's real fear was that Javidan was in custody.

According to the Criminal Code of Georgia, for Gizo Khomeriki waited sentenced to many years in prison, because he was charged with the following crimes: – Life assault, premeditated murder, ordering murder, unlawful possession, and manufacture of firearms. As the other accomplices of the assassination were liquidated for disobedience to the police, Suliko Jankhoteli was at the edge of death and Sergi Menabde was not fully informed, so Gizo Khomeriki decided to violate his right to remain silent and to give the prosecution full testimony. Amongst them, he would have to admit the crime he had planned. He was the organizer of kidnapping the mother of four, in the necessity to defend themselves to the Kalandadze house roof. There also expected severe punishment for the two prisoners already in custody for taking the hostage ... and using that hostage to force the prosecution to fulfill their promise. The crime was punishable under the Criminal Code of Georgia.

REVEALED SINS

Mamia Zirakishvili left the General Prosecutor's Office. He remembered that it was necessary to have conversation with Londa Amilakhvari.

Londa seemed to have aged by ten years. She looked exhausted, insomniac and bottomlessly sad. She respected, loved and trusted Mamia immensely. Every job was entrusted to him. As soon as she heard Mamia's voice, she cheered up. Mamia was a decent and professional person, and it was a reason, why Londa trusted him mostly. After a rather warm talk, Mamia advised Londa to add another experienced investigator lado Mikaberidze to this case, a very trustful and honest man as well, as he alone would not be able to interrogate such an important criminal, like Gizo Khomeriki. Londa agreed with Mamia's proposal and decided to add Lado Mikaberidze to the group. This was indeed the moment when the investigation needed special caution, namely: two eyes, two ears, and one common heart. Khomeriki was a major offender and also a military police officer with many years of experience.

On the way Lado and Mamia came into the conversation. They blamed Khomeriki for disregarding the moral code and violating his uniform. What concerned the serial offenses he committed, this was aggravating the subject of investigation. Most of all, they were interested in Gizo Khomeriki opinion.

Lado recalled Immanuel Kant's statement: "Man must come out of a tight personal frame. It must do so that the highest principle of its will is always to have the force, strength of universal law."

Our behavior, my Mamia, must really be the norm of universal law.

Lado continued, – then we'll be real professionals.

Mamia's heart believed that these standards were respected by Lado. He glanced silently at his youth time past and remembered Gigi Papinashvili, one of the best friend of his youth, who was truly uplifted on moral base, and he remembered also many other close friends ... and he remembered the proverb: "Tell me who your friend is and I will tell you who you are."

With these thoughts, Mamia calmed down, looked at Lado, and read the same thought on his face.

Meanwhile they arrived at Digomi. Gizo Khomeriki's lawyers – Zurab Rostiashvili and Mamuka Nozadze, were at the entrance to the police station – serious lawyers with extensive experience.

Gizo Khomeriki looked restless. It looked extremely tired and sleepless. Who knows what kind fires were burning in his young heart. He was obviously clearly suffering from the crimes, committed by him. Unfortunately, no one would ask him, could he avoid these crimes or not: or was it all his own addiction, since he could always correct the situation. Moreover, he skillfully managed to continue the crime in order to cover up the murder of Mirza Kurdiani.

Lado Mikaberidze started questioning:

Since when do you work in the Ministry of Defense? – Since 1989.

Who have you been assigned to recommend?

At the recommendation of my closest friend Gaga Jankhoteli. – If you remember when you met Gaga and in what circumstances?

I knew his brother Suliko Jankhoteli and he introduced me.

Do you know that Jankhoteli was injured, wounded and he is in the hospital?

Yes, I know.

Who wounded Suliko Jankhoteli, don't you know? – As far as I know, he tried to kill himself.

For what reason? Do you know what was happening at the end of his life?

He had no private life, his family collapsed and he fell into big business debts, despite being a major stakeholder in the casino.

Do you have any personal contact with Gaga or you contacted with him through Suliko?

Primary relationships, of course ... We had more in common than me and Suliko.

What did you have in common, or what secrets did you have? – Of course, human secrets that I can never say.

What do you mean by personal secrets and human moments that you were asked or passed on?

He couldn't order me because he was in another job and he was requesting, asking me.

And you did it too, didn't you? – Mamia Zirakishvili got involved.

It was not only his request. He was instructed too.

How would you like to comply? How exactly would he instruct you?

Then I will say what I could not do.

Well, sir, you said, what request did you not make? You probably know that you are accused of killing Mirza Kurdiani.

Then I tell you that I did not fulfill that request.

Who did it and at what cost? You know, if you tell the truth, the sentence will be lessened and you will get less punishment.

Of course, I know ... I would like to tell you that I did not know Mirza Kurdiani and I had no account with him.

Why, why did Gaga Jankhoteli asked you to liquidate Mirza, they were colleagues and they had a lot in common?

Yes, I agree with you... they had many share interests to go with it, but Mr. Mirza radically opposed the "law thieves" and day– and– night wondered how to destroy this dark world.

What role were you in? As we know, you had no competence in the workplace, so you could neither help nor hinder it.

I agree, but I was entrusted with control from the police chief, and Gaga Jankhoteli sent me the "scissors" and I got into a terrible state after that.

What was your relationship with "Scissors"?

However, I have had two different wounds at different times from him. He categorically asked for assistance in the liquidation of some senior prosecutors.

Who's liquidation specifically he requested?

In particular, they decided to get rid of Mirza Kurdiani. – Who did he plan it with?

Is there a thief, Kukusha. – Only "Kukusha?"

No, "scissors" too.

As it seems, he does not know about his friend's liquidation in Turkey, do not let him know it yet.

Mamia told quietly to Lado.

Do you know who is Sergi Menabde and why he is in the prison?

Well, I know he was my employee.

How? did you give him a cleaning jobs? – No, he is a military person, an officer.

Why such a man should work as a cleaner? who was paying him his salary?

He had money problems and I offered to pay him salary. We didn't tell him that we needed it for our plans, from the starting that we needed agents. Then Gaga Jankhoteli summoned him and asked him to do a good job for the police. He would definitely receive a remuneration for this. It was all about... Sergo was only tasked with tracking down to watch specific individuals. On the contrary, we were telling him that we needed all the information he had obtained to protect Solomon Kalandadze's interests. So, Sergi is a decent, but financially needy, poor man. He does not have any guilt.

How? Did not he deliver the explosives to a minor?

No, he only brought a letter for him, nothing more.

Who shot Mirza Kurdiani?

Gaga Jankhoteli knows his name. – Do not you know him?

No, one thing I can tell you is that he is a military person, a sniper, he killed him for money.

Did you meet him?

Yes, I can recognize him.

Who knows him besides you? – Only Gaga Jankhoteli.

Have you seen them together?

Yes, they were planning the murder.

And were not you afraid of the result of it?

They didn't give me time to think, I had many assignments.

Specifically, I was commissioned to spy on Kalandadze, or rather the members of the Kalandadze's family. Initially they were planning to liquidate, they wanted to get rid of investigator Londa Amilakhvari too with my own hand, but they realized that I would not do it.

We will need you for identification purposes recognition! – I agree.

But I request a detailed description of that person.

Gizo Khomeriki described exactly the same picture as Solomon Kalandadze, one difference being that Gizo Khomeriki knew his exact age – 32 years old – so he said, and Kalandadze didn't know his age and mentioned 25– 27 years old.

Why could not you implement your plans with regard to these individuals and why not get rid of those who knew this?

They were planning, but did not dare to finish the case, moreover, they wanted to kill the killer, the "sniper", to get rid of him, but he fled abroad. Had he been here, he would not have left Solomon Kalandadze alive as a witness.

When was border crossed? – A month after the murder.

What was the threat, or how did you know they were threatened?

The law thieves wanted to kill him, Kukusha and "Scissors" could not trust him to the end.

Is it true that the killer used to play gambling?

Yes, I know that he lost a lot of money in Suliko Jankhoteli's casino.

How much?

15,000 USD and failed to pay, after which they suggested the murder of Mirza Kurdiani.

Although he had not played before, but the Jankoteli brothers encouraged him to win and gave him some money to play. He won the minimum sum and entered the gamble. Then they encouraged him to ply for larger sums and he lost it all, so, selling the house was inevitable. As I know, he even tried to kill himself. It was then that they emerged as rescuers and offered to think again about this proposal. He thought a lot and agreed with this cruel proposal. I still think that they were forced to do this horror if they had to face the witness, and if he were a killer, he would kill him, even if it was to cover his tracks.

You're wrong here, he had seven bullets fired and Mirza Kurdiani shot dead with three bullets, it was just Kalandadze's fate, because the killer finished with bullets, otherwise he would shot him.

I am hearing it for the first time. as the Jankhotelis reprimanded him about not killing the witness, the killer replied that he had been paid for killing only for one man and that why would kill another one.

I see.

You probably know that "scissors" is in prison.

I don't know, I thought they escaped? That's fine, He has done a lot of bad things, but it's good. Kukusha is much better than him, he is not aggressive at any rate.

Gizo Khomeriki felt bad. The desire to speak was lost and he demanded water. It was as if he doubled the gravity of his crime during questioning.

"Can we finish today?" asked Khomeriki in a low voice.

"Of course, do you need a doctor?" Mamia asked.

No, I don't want to think about anything else. – I have one request.

Could you tell me if Ms. Javidani is in custody?

Our answer is no, Javidan Tarkhun will be questioned as a witness. She is not detained.

I understand, thank you. Gizo Khomeriki breathed a sigh of relief.

Mamia Zirakishvili and Lado Mikaberidze said farewell to Gizo's lawyers and went to the prosecutor's office with satisfaction.

A SENSATIONAL STORY

A team of investigators, led by Londa, assembled again. This time, not empty information, but they had serious reports. They knew a lot already, some quietly, some clearly. They tried to study the witness, Gizo Khomeriki, at the end of the testimony, wondering how sincere he was. But the fact was that his testimony coincided with the testimony of other witnesses.

The main two things were: the recovery of Suliko Jankhoteli and the detailed study of Gaga Jankhoteli's environment.

The fact was that they were second– rate gunmen ... Three criminals were killed in the city of Samsun; the killer of Mirza Qurdiani had escaped abroad. The criminals on the roof of Mirza Kurdiani's house were questioned, but unfortunately they did not provide any new information, apparently in fear of the Jankhoteli brothers.

The Jankhoteli brothers behaved almost like an undefeated fortress. By order of Londa Amilakhvari, Dudu Arziani had to go to the hospital to Suliko Jankhoteli. Dudu decided to find out from Vep-khia Lomidze Suliko's condition and went there. When he arrived there, he saw that tired Vepkhia stood at the window and watched with regret the ambulance, coming to take Suliko Jankhoteli's body to post– mortem section. The secretary informed him, that he had a guest, the doctor was waiting for his visitor in an opened doorway. Dudu asked to Vepkhia, what was going on, why he was looking so unhappy: "Is there peace?" – Worried Vepkhia responded him, that Suliko Jankhoteli died of anemia at 11am. This information was so unexpected, that the worried investigator put his hand to his heart and ran out ... "Another person" ... – Arziani cried out. Vepkhia followed him out and said: "We gave lots of attention to him, but in last days he had been struggling with life in vain".

The investigators attended the postmortem of the corpse. The cause of death appeared to be identical to the diagnosis.

***

The funeral of Suliko Jankhoteli passed without any excesses. The operative service watched the process and produced video footage. The investigation had already created a photo– fit of the killer. The funeral was attended by many people. Although the witness, Mamuka Akhalkatsi, named Jaba as the direct killer, the prosecution was still unable to establish who the person was.

On the day of the funeral, because of the sunny weather, the criminal investigation did a great job, and it worked. Initially, investigations amongst coming youth suspected only the person, who were bringing photo of Suliko Jankhoteli. The ceremony was attended by the leadership of the police. Londa was also here with the prosecutors. She was inspecting everything around her... She as if was hearing humiliating, degrading laugh of murderers of Mirza Qurdiani... She was losing her peace.

The strange situation was raging. People of all ranks gathered around: Thieves in law, police chefs, military police, defense ministry officials and the Office of the Prosecutor General ... It seemed as if the deplorable condition of helpless Georgia was worse by the mourning of the relatives of deceived man. As if mother was crying not for just for her gone astray lost son, but she was grieving of the full fate of Georgia.

THE KILLER IS DISCOVERED

The investigation team decided to interrogate Giga Jankhoteli. It should have happened on the third day after the funeral. But before that, they had begun to look at the video or photo material they had obtained at the funeral. The young men in uniforms were the first to arrive. One of them, whose appearance coincided with the data described by Solomon Kalandadze, was wearing a military– style coat and a so– called military boots. He had black sunglasses on... One of the militaries, beside him, was identified as an employee of the Ministry of Defense. The person was summoned to the Prosecutor's Office to identify the suspect. He looked at the photograph and identified Jaba Gorgiladze, wearing black glasses and a jacket, he was walking in front of funeral procession, and he also recognized all the military personnel who were in the forefront.

Are you convinced? – Londa asked.

Yes, lady! – He answered with a modest voice.

Can you write on the paper personal details of the people in the photograph and sign on it with confirming your identity.

Yes, of course.

The witness gave the names of all the employees, including Jaba Gorgiladze. He added information to Jaba and said that he had been abroad for a while and only arrived at the funeral, because he was Suliko's and Gaga's closest friend. When Jaba lost a large sum of money and even attempted to kill himself, Suliko and Giga came to his aid and paid him in full. After that, Jaba did not move away from them.

How did you learn all about it?

Certainly from Jaba, because we knew Suliko from him. – Did not you know Gaga?

No, I have never met him. I knew from Jaba, that Suliko's brother was a senior police officer.

Upon hearing this information, Dudu Arziani went to the side and rang to the airport to call to find out whether Jaba Gorgiladze had crossed the border or not. They inspected all borders of Georgia and found no crossings. Fortunately, he was still in Georgia.

The photo was also shown to Solomon Kalandadze, who identified Jaba amongst ten people.

The investigation had almost reached the final stage. Today or tomorrow Mirza Qurdiani's murderers would be on the accused chair. Investigation procedures needed to continue working for the main culprit, Gaga Jankhoteli, and, who knows, how many other cases would be it covered, as it was the criminal group made up of people of different mentalities? A mafia gang was trying to strengthen itself. They were formed in the complicated early 90s. Then all people were focused on saving themselves. All the cowardice then emerged: Gambling, only to be seen in the movies by young people, was now easily accessible to them. Most of them were dragged into the gambling, and in the event of a loss they even had to sell their homes to bring the lost money back to the thieves. otherwise if they could not pay money, they had to deal with a case that often ended with their physical elimination. Yes, they were meeting with thieves who were gathering with Suliko and Gaga Jankhotelis. Yes, exactly with these thieves, as they were deciding the fate of humans and also fate of the whole country.

Marauders and pillagers, dressed in uniforms and pretended as heroes themselves, called themselves "Mkhedrioni", and other the same kind of groups, staffed with people of uncertain mentality, robbed civilians. People dressed in military uniforms were so misconstrued that mothers would warn their children, that they would not trust any military man.

... And, finally, even the murder of a senior prosecutor official was decided and even carried out.

CRYING OF JACKALS

Jaba has found the best shelter in the village of Gudaleti in the Kaspi region. This village is a forest zone and the inhabitants rarely live there. Most of the shepherds live here because they have good pastures.

Jaba was dressed appropriately and began to rush into the woods around the village, as if he was a soil scientist, studying the composition of the land. The Shepherds were watching from afar. One of them approached him and asked:

What are you doing here?

Jaba explained that he was studying the soil.

Have you been busy with this case for a long time?

Yes, it's the eighth year I've been designing seismic zones.

Aaa? I see.

What are you doing, are you alone here? – Asked Jaba.

No, I'm not alone, I'm with my friend Janri. We feed the sheep flock.

How? does not the population live here?

They arrive at the cottages seasonally and no one is here this time of year anymore, except us. Jaba noticed, that the boy had been startled and confused. He also made doubt another factor that the young boy was dressed in military style striped T– shirt and the soldier's boots on his feet.

The boy apologized and chased the fleeing sheep.

Jaba could not remember, what was the shepherd's name, the boy mentioned. would be for Henry or Janri, he went to the shipman's hut. He checked his personal papers in his jacket pocket again and calmed down. Everything was in its place.

"Janri!" – Jaba called.

Janri was sitting on the three leg stool and was rolling tobacco. He stretched his hand passing him a box of tobacco and advised

it him wholeheartedly:

If you smoke, take as much as you want.

–Yes, I do, thanks for the suggestion, but I'm smoking Marlboro. Jaba took out a pack of cigarettes from his backpack and gave him as a gift.

That is how the friendship of the wanted Gorgiladze started with the shepherds. Shepherds were not ashamed with the guest, and offered him cover and some food and vodka. They started drinking. Appeared, that Janri had graduated from Polytechnic Institute, but could not find any job for this profile and was now working as a sheppard in this deep deserted forest. What concerned the second shepherd, he was not staying in the hut, was going every minute out, as if, outside was danger and he was checking it. It got twilight and Jaba took out from his back– pack a soft, striped T– shirt and put it on.

They were talking frankly... Jaba noticed that Janri was well educated young man. He expressed his surprise that the second shepherd did not seem so friendly and wondered why he was not coming close to him.

After a little thought, Janry explained that the shepherd was afraid of the boy coming to them.

Why, why he frightened of me? – Jaba asked surprisingly.

I'll tell you one secret and don't reveal it,– whispered Janri. – I'm grave, trust me. – Gorgiladze was pleased.

This guy was serving in the army, could not stand the regime there and ran away, now is hiding with me.

Why he was scared of me?

He recognised you, he said that you were working in army.

Has he mixed me up with someone else?

No, he recognised you straight away and said that your name is Jaba.

Jaba was not pleased hearing this. but he kept himself calm...

Jaba? I know one guy is in the army as an officer, and I think this guy is right, I really look like him.

What is your name and surname? – I am Johnny Kaikatsishvili.

What a great surname you have, to be honest, I have never heard of that surname.

Tell me true, you are looking for this guy?

Jaba was embarrassed... he was not worrying about the boy. He had his own problem... He realised that he was in some trouble. Maybe the boy knows his last name... and suddenly, he went into an ultimatum:

"Well, I swear, I will never mention you nowhere and you promise not to mention me, that you ever have seen me. Okey?" Jaba said delightfully.

They were in this arrangement but the boy no longer seemed to come.

"Where is the boy?" Jaba asked angrily.

Below is Ezatia, a small village, he has got relatives there, he would probably run there.

Jaba did not want Janri to notice his excitement about it, and pretending as if nothing had happened, added a glass of vodka and demanded a hand– held radio. The host provided a slice of barbecue and a glass of vodka for two and a half hours, turned on the radio at the last sound and asked him to forget what had happened.

Yes, in Ezat – who are his relatives, don't you know? – Well, there are Tsivilashvili.

Tsivilashvili? is it the man who works in the police?

No, it is not him. This man is trying to became a "Law thief". They are called "Achain".

On hearing this, Jaba Gorgiladze got calmer and relaxed. It was a dark night, he could not go anywhere and trusted his fate.

There was so little space in the hut that it would be said: "The mouse wouldn't catch its tail." He went outside and after little walking, decided to ask for a coat from Janri to lie outside on. For a while, he was smoking cigarettes and checking his roundabouts. He could not feel any danger from anywhere. Just from afar was hearing crying of jackals. Near the hut he collected wood chips and dried beech branches and lit a fire. He looked in the hut and saw deeply asleep Janri.

There, on the floor, he saw a coat, took it out, spread it and lay on it. He put his back–pack next to him and started looking at the stars.

Jaba recently often was alone, but never was left alone in the open air with the stars, but he had no feelings now, he felt that he lived on instinct, he could no longer connect with the skies, he was on the animal level and the stars appeared for him to be on fire. Moreover, he also had a sense of fear... yes, insurmountable fear. He thought one of the stars would come down and burn him.

Though after little thinking, he guessed that he was not afraid of that fire, because he felt like the last person and was ready to go to hell.

From the moment Jaba committed the crime, he was eager to get far, far away from his homeland. Even if could never had been known, who the killer was. He had a terrible desire to hide and not to perceive himself. Though he had been in the capital city for at least a month after the killing. If he had fallen asleep at night, the nightmares would have awaken him, and he had desire to either surrender to the police and confess, or he would run too far.

Solomon Kalandadze and his frustrated face was

constantly following him everywhere. Sometimes he regretted leaving him alive, he sometimes thought himself as a hero, that he did not kill him. He didn't kill or could not kill him? He was always on the verge of answering this question? No one ordered him to kill another person. Why not kill him in the second case? If it could not be sustained. He possessed, all bullets were shot in front of Solomon to Mirza Kurdiani. This topic, all life, would probably remain unanswered, it was premature to answer, because the results of the murder, of this horrible crime, were not yet established, even though the investigation was in a very active phase, even the killer had not been identified yet. Following the killer, they were wondering, where could be hidden Jaba Gorgiladze.

... In the meantime he fell asleep.

The cold feeling and strange voices woke him up in the middle of the night. He suddenly noticed that he was surrounded by jackals and he was in the middle of a circle. They unexpectedly invaded him. If not Janri, He would not manage to free himself from them and they would tear him in pieces. Janri took him inside, lit a fire, boiled water, and treated the wounds with vodka. Then Jaba took off his sports pants and changed old one and put on his own top, above. He was exhausted from fighting with jackals, soon he fell asleep again. In the morning Janri's screaming woke him, he realized that Janri was grazing the sheep. He decided to sneak off away. Soon Janri came to the hut and asked him: "Jaba, brother, do you need anything?"

Jaba didn't make a sound. He pretended to be asleep. He had already planned on how to escape, feeling completely emptied of faith. He felt so horrible... He was following with his eyes Janri's movement...

After a short time, Jaba escaped from there with great soul and physical pains, but in spite of it, he was still running down the rural road.

A DESPERATE SHEPHERD

As soon as he found free time, Janry headed to the hut again. Suddenly, front of him something reddened. He approached it and found out Jaba's documents, scattered there... From the night's fight they were being blown by the wind. He collected the papers one by one and ran to the hut. He was surprised, when he looked at Johnny's military– style photo, he brought it close to his eyes and looked at it again... Yes, it was Johnny and it was definitely a military man... Doubt captured Janry, that Johnny definitely was sent to them to find out about The boy. When he checked his passport, he discovered, that he was not Johnny Kaikacishvili, as he said, but he was Jaba Gorgiladze, a military man, and had an invitation to travel abroad in Ivanovo, Russia.

Janry read the invitation document carefully and wrote down the identity of the invitee. At the same time, all the important moments of the document were copied, the papers were scribbled in the newspaper and kept well. Outside, he collected Jaba's torn blood-soaked clothes and hats and placed them in a black plastic bag.

Janry was thinking of the Jabas phenomenon. If he had an invitation to Russia, why he was wandering here and was digging the ground. He has the invitation even within a week, what would a week– long trip man was doing in the Caspian village, Gudaleti forest. It is obvious, that he was looking for Ramin, the boy that run from the military service. He betrayed us, asking us even for a night shelter.

By the minute, the police will arrive here and will request me all information about Ramin. "What can I do now?" – Soon after, he decided to go to Ezat village with these documents and find something. He was well aware that criminal responsibility for covering up the crime would be addressed to him, so he had to take all the documents and file them with the police. Only he did not know what to do with the sheep. He remembered the shepherds in the second pasture and fled there hoping that the sheep would one day be delivered. Janry's hopes were approved, the good shepherds took over the flock of sheep and Janry was released for a day.

Janry arrived in the village of Ezat. He found the Tsivilashvili's district, where Tsivilashvili's tribe lived, and he approached to a two– storey house. As he did not know the real name of the host he called for Ramin. There were not any sounds. Janri tried and called several times. An elderly woman came out from the yard next door, telling him the boy to be taken to the police. Upon hearing this, Janri was bothered very much. He realized that he was in a great trouble and decided to visit the Kaspi district prosecutor.

Prosecutor Gulbat Besiashvili met him on the spot the same day with deep attention, and when he heard everything, he could not hide his excitement. He praised Janry that he was very brave man.

Jaba Gorgiladze's documents were added to the case and they rushed to the capital city. Janry could not guess what was delighting the prosecutor so much and decided to ask him to return Ramini to army without any punishment. The prosecutor was agreed for that. Before Gulbat Besiashvili left for Tbilisi, he took operative measures to find Jaba Gorgiladze. In all villages around Gudaleti they were actively searching for him.

Jaba Gorgiladze was detained in the village of Idleti and taken to a pre– trial detention center in Tbilisi.

UNIFICATION OF BLOOD LAW CASES

Long years of hard work by Londa Amilakhvari and her team members was finally appreciated. Four prisoners were revealed for case of killed prosecutor Mirza Kurdiani, and Gaga Jankhoteli were summoned for questioning. The man was considered operative by the order of the current Prosecutor General of Georgia Nikoloz Gabrichidze and was being watched.

Gaga Jankhoteli was summoned by Dudu Arziani for questioning. After some hesitation, Gaga agreed to testify. In the room where Jankhoteli was questening, Dudu set the windows down with iron– plated shields and created the environment for the high– level police officer to read in a calm environment.

Gaga looked pretty exasperated. He could barely move out a chair ... but he was not going to sit on it.

Sit down, Mr. Gaga, and tell me what you know about the murder of Mirza Kurdiani.

Mirza Kurdiani was an excellent person, but was killed anyway ...

What kind of person was he, it is no matter now, if he had been a bad person, would it be killed?

No, please, understand me correctly, I would like to say that despite the fact that he was a good person and honest prosecutor, he was still killed.

Who killed him and under what circumstances, you probably know?

The investigator turned the tap on to pour water. Gaga stepped up, and asked to be escorted to the necessary room.

Dudu gave him a glass of water and asked: – Do you feel unwell?

No, I had high blood pressure in the morning and got some medicine, can you take me out?

Ok, no another way, – said Dudu and instructed the security guard there to be careful.

Unfortunately, Gaga did not get out of the toilet because he jumped from the fourth floor through the open window.

The body of Gaga Jankhoteli was transported to the Prosecutor's Office by ambulance.

INTERROGATION OF JABA GORGILADZE

Goga and Dudu got ready to interrogate Jaba Gorgiladze, but in vain... Jaba Gorgiladze chose the right to remain silent, he really had the right to choose silence by law. So he chose to meet in silence with the charges against him and the court ruling.

SOME TIME HAS PASSED....

The case of Jaba Gorgiladze and Gizo Khomeriki was heard in the sixth chamber of the Supreme Court Prosecutor Londa Ami-lakhvari, victim's lawyer Rusudan Meshveliani and three attorneys for the accused. The trial was led by Jemal Leonidze, a member of the Supreme Court panel.

The court found the verdict lawful. The murderer and the accomplice in the murder were sentenced to the penal code of Georgia!

Yes! – the sentence, that was not appealed by either sides!!!

INDEX